"I don't want to like you too much,"

she said softly, struggling to express herself.
"That would only complicate a nice, serene
relationship. We're having such a good time and I
don't want to ruin it."

"In other words you don't want to fall in love with
me?"

"Exactly." Carla hated the heartless way this
made her sound. Already she recognized that
falling for Philip wouldn't be difficult.

"Don't you think you're overreacting just a little
to the fact I'm a policeman?" Philip asked, his
voice restrained and searching.

"It's not going to work, Philip. Not for another
day. Not for a week. Not at all. I'm going back to
the hotel."

"Carla, will you listen to me." Philip's face
hardened with a grimness she hadn't expected.
"You're already involved."

Dear Reader,

Although our culture is always changing, the desire to love and be loved is a constant in every woman's heart. Silhouette Romances reflect that desire, sweeping you away with books that will make you laugh and cry, poignant stories that will move you time and time again.

This year we're featuring Romances with a playful twist. Remember those fun-loving heroines who always manage to get themselves into tricky predicaments? You'll enjoy reading about their escapades in Silhouette Romances by Brittany Young, Debbie Macomber, Annette Broadrick and Rita Rainville.

We're also publishing Romances by many of your all-time favorites such as Ginna Gray, Dixie Browning, Laurie Paige and Joan Hohl. Your overwhelming reaction to these authors has served as a touchstone for us, and we're pleased to bring you more books with Silhouette's distinctive medley of charm, wit and—above all—*romance*. I hope you enjoy this book, and the many stories to come.

Sincerely,

Rosalind Noonan
Senior Editor
SILHOUETTE BOOKS

DEBBIE MACOMBER
Shadow
Chasing

Silhouette Romance

Published by Silhouette Books New York

America's Publisher of Contemporary Romance

SILHOUETTE BOOKS
300 E. 42nd St., New York, N.Y. 10017

ISBN: 0-373-08415-3

First Silhouette Books printing February 1986

America's Publisher of Contemporary Romance

Printed in the U.S.A.

Books by Debbie Macomber

Silhouette Special Edition

Starlight #128
Borrowed Dreams #241
Reflections of Yesterday #284

Silhouette Romance

That Wintery Feeling #316
Promise Me Forever #341
Adam's Image #349
The Trouble with Caasi #379
A Friend or Two #392
Christmas Masquerade #405
Shadow Chasing #415

DEBBIE MACOMBER

has quickly become one of Silhouette's most prolific authors. As a wife and mother of four, she not only manages to keep her family happy, but she also keeps her publisher and readers happy with each book she writes.

Chapter One

You're kidding." Carla Walker glanced at her friend suspiciously. "What did they put in that margarita, anyway? Sodium pentothal?"

Nancy Listten's dark eyes brightened, but her attention didn't waver from the mariachi band that played softly in the background.

"I'm not," Nancy replied. "This happens every vacation. We now have seven glorious days in Mazatlán. What do you want to bet that we don't find a man until day six?"

"That's because it takes awhile to scout out who's available," Carla argued, taking a sip of her drink. The granules of salt from the edge of the glass felt gritty on the inside of her bottom lip. But she enjoyed the feel and the taste.

"Exactly my point."

Nancy took off her glasses and placed them inside her purse. That action said a lot. Her friend was serious, dead serious.

"We spend at least two days trying to figure out who's married and who isn't."

"Your idea isn't going to help," Carla insisted. "The next two men who walk in here could be married."

"But imagine how much time it'll save if we *ask*. And"—Nancy inhaled a deep breath—"have you noticed how picky we are? We always act like our choices are going to improve if given enough time. We've simply got to realize that there're no better candidates than whoever walks through that door tonight."

"I don't know..." Carla hesitated, wondering if there was something wrong with her drink, too. Nancy's idea was beginning to make sense. "What if they speak Spanish?" That was a stupid question, and the look Nancy gave her said as much. They each had a phrase book, and Carla had watched enough *Sesame Street* when baby-sitting her nieces to pick up the basics of the language. She groaned inwardly. She'd begun this vacation with such high hopes. Seven glorious days in one of the most popular vacation spots in the world. Men galore. Rich men. And she was going to end up introducing herself in *Sesame Street* Spanish to the next guy who walked through the door. Even worse, the idea was growing more appealing by the minute. Nancy was right. For two years they'd ruined their vacations looking for Mr. Perfect. Not only hadn't they ever found him, but as their time had grown shorter, their standards had lowered. The men they'd found marginal on day one looked like rare finds by day six. And on day seven, frustrated and discouraged, they'd flown back to Seattle.

"I think we should establish some sort of criteria, don't you?"

Carla nodded. "Unencumbered."

"That goes without saying." Nancy gave her a classroom glare that Carla had seen often enough to recognize. "They should walk in here alone. And be under thirty-five." Nancy's eyes sought Carla. "Anything else?"

"I, for one, happen to be a little more particular than you."

"All right, add what you want."

"I think they should order a margarita."

"Carla! We could be here all night if we did that."

"We're in Mazatlán; everyone orders margaritas," Carla countered. Well, a tourist would and that was what she wanted. No serious stuff, just a nice holiday romance.

"Okay," Nancy agreed.

Their eyes focused on the two entrances. Waiting.

"Have you noticed how all the cocktail lounges are beginning to look like Levitz showrooms?" Carla commented, just to have something to say. Her hands felt damp.

"Shh...someone's coming."

A middle-aged couple walked through the door.

They relaxed. "We'd better decide who goes first."

"You," Carla returned instantly. "It was your idea."

"All right," she agreed, and straightened, nervously folding her hands on her lap.

Carla pulled up the spaghetti strap to her pink summer dress. Normally a redhead couldn't wear pink, but this shade, the color of camellias, complemented the unusual color of her hair.

"Here comes a single man."

Two pairs of intense eyes followed the lumbering gait of a dark-haired Latin-American who entered the lounge and took the closest available love seat.

"He's in a cast," Nancy observed in a high-pitched whisper.

"Don't panic," Carla said in a reassuring tone. "He doesn't look like the type to order a margarita."

Nancy opened her purse and put on her glasses. "Not bad-looking, though."

"Yes, I suppose so," Carla agreed, although she thought he looked too much like Erik Estrada to suit her. His toothy smile looked bright enough to blind someone in broad daylight. For Nancy's sake, she hoped Mr. Chips was into wine coolers. "You can back out if you want," Carla said, almost wishing Nancy would. The whole idea was crazy.

"Not on your life."

"The guy's in a cast up to his hip. I'd say he was encumbered, wouldn't you?"

"No," Nancy replied smoothly. "You're doing it again."

"Doing what?"

"You know."

"All right, I'll shut up. If you want to be stuck with a guy who leaves a funny trail in the sand, that's fine with me."

"Look," Nancy whispered, "your fellow's arrived."

Quickly, Carla's attention focused on the lounge entrance at the other side of the room. She recognized him immediately as someone from the same flight as theirs. Not that she'd found him particularly interesting at the time. He'd sat across the aisle from Nancy and read a book during the entire trip.

"Hey, he was on the plane with us," Nancy pointed out.

"I know," Carla answered evenly, trying to disguise her disappointment. Secretly, she'd been hoping for someone compelling and forcefully masculine. She should have known better.

Both girls sat in rigid silence as their eyes followed the young cocktail waitress, who delivered two margaritas, one to Chips, and one to the bookworm.

"You ready?" Nancy whispered.

"What are we going to say?" Carla's hand tightened around her purse.

Nancy gave another of those glares normally reserved for her pupils. "Good grief, Carla, we're mature women. We know what to say."

Carla shook her head. "Mature women wouldn't do something like this."

They stood together, condemned prisoners marching to the hangman's noose. "How do I look?" Nancy asked with a weak smile.

"Like you're about to throw up."

Her friend briefly closed her eyes. "That's the way I feel."

Carla hesitated.

"Come on," Nancy hissed. "We aren't backing out now."

Carla couldn't believe that calm, level-headed, left-brained Nancy would actually suggest something like this. It was completely out of character. Carla was the impulsive one—creative, imaginative, right-brained. That was why they were such good friends: their personalities complemented each other perfectly. Right-brained, left-brained, Carla mused. That was the problem. Each of them had only half a brain.

She studied the man from the plane. He wasn't anyone she would normally have sought out. For a light romance, she wanted someone more dynamic. This guy was decidedly—she searched for the right word—undashing. He was tall, she remembered, which was lucky. At five nine she didn't look up to many men. And he was on the lanky side. Almost reedy. He wore horn-rimmed glasses, which gave him a serious look. His sandy hair, parted on the side, fell carelessly across his wide brow. His tan was rich, but Carla mused that he didn't look like the type to use a tanning machine or lie lazily in the sun. He probably worked outdoors—maybe he was a mailman.

He glanced at her and smiled. Carla nearly tripped on the plush carpet. His eyes were fantastic. A deep gray like the overcast winter clouds with the sun beaming through. A brilliant silver shade that she had never seen. Her spirits brightened; the man's eyes, at least, were encouragingly attractive.

"Hello," she said as she stood in front of his deep cushioned chair. "I'm Carla Walker." She extended her hand. Might as well be forthright about this.

He stood, dwarfing her by a good four inches, and shook hands. "Philip Garrison."

He looked like a Philip. "We were on the same airplane, weren't we?"

He pushed his glasses up the bridge of his nose with his index finger. The action reminded her of Clark Kent. But Carla wasn't kidding herself—Philip Garrison was no Superman.

"I believe we were," he said with a smile that was surprisingly compelling. "Would you like to sit down?"

"Yes, thank you." Carla took the chair beside him. Hoping to give an impression of nonchalance, she crossed her shapely legs. "Are you from Seattle?"

"Spokane."

"On vacation?"

His smile deepened the grooves along the edges of his mouth. "In a way. My parents have a condominium here that needs a few repairs."

Carla smiled absently into her drink. So he was a carpenter. The occupation suited him, she decided. He was deceptively lean and muscular. And he had a subtle, understated appeal, something she found refreshing.

"Would you like another margarita?" he asked as he glanced at her empty glass.

"Yes. Thank you."

He raised his hand to get the waitress's attention. The lovely olive-skinned girl acknowledged his gesture and indicated that she would be there in a moment. Service here was notoriously slow, but right now Carla didn't mind. She looked around for Nancy and discovered that her friend was chatting easily and seemed to be enjoying herself. At the moment, this crazy scheme appeared to be working beautifully.

"Is this your first visit to Mazatlán?" Philip asked, and took a sip of his drink.

Carla noted the way the tip of his tongue eased the salt from the bottom of his lip. She dropped her gaze, finding his action disturbingly provocative. "Yes, this is my first time in Mexico. To be honest, I didn't expect it to be this beautiful."

The waitress arrived, and Carla handed the girl her empty glass. She had noticed that the waitresses spoke only minimal English. Although her Spanish wasn't terrific, the urge to impress Philip with her knowledge of the language overpowered her good sense, so, proudly, without the hint of a foreign accent, Carla asked for another drink.

The waitress frowned and glanced at Philip, who was obviously trying to contain his laughter. He delivered a crisp request to the girl, who nodded and smiled before turning away.

"What's so humorous?" Carla could feel herself blushing.

Philip composed himself quickly. "You just told the waitress that Big Bird wants a drink of water."

Carla closed her eyes and did her best to laugh, but the sound was weak and revealing. She would never watch *Sesame Street* again, she vowed, no matter how desperate she was to entertain her two nieces.

"How long will you be staying?" he asked pleasantly, deftly changing the subject.

"A week. My roommate, Nancy, and I are on a discount vacation package for teachers."

"You teach preschool?"

It was a logical assumption. "No, I'm a surgical assistant."

One thick brow arched with surprise. "You don't look much older than a student yourself."

"I'm twenty-two." And old enough to know better than to make a fool of myself like this, she added silently.

Their drinks arrived, and Carla restrained the urge to gulp hers down and ease the parched feeling in her throat. Gradually she relaxed as they spoke about the flight and the weather.

After a half hour of exchanging pleasantries, Philip asked her if she was available to join him for dinner. The invitation pleased her. Since her faux pas with the waitress, she'd imagined he'd wanted to be rid of her.

"Yes, I'd like that very much." To her surprise, Carla discovered it was the truth.

He took her to a restaurant named El Marinero. The view of the harbor was excellent, as was the shrimp dinner. Philip spoke to the waiter in Spanish, then quietly translated for Carla. It was a thoughtful gesture. She would have felt excluded otherwise. Not once did he try to overwhelm her with his wit and charm. He was who he was, quiet and a little reserved, and apparently he saw no need to change because he'd been approached by her.

"I can't believe I ate that much," Carla groaned as they left the restaurant. The air was still sultry but much cooler than when they'd arrived.

"Would you like to walk along the beach? It'll be less crowded outside the hotel."

"I'd love to." Her blue eyes looked fondly into his. "But can we? I mean, it's all privately owned, isn't it?"

"Not in Mexico. The beaches are for everyone."

"How nice," Carla murmured, thinking she was beginning to like Philip more with every passing minute.

They rode back to the hotel in an open-air vehicle that resembled a golf cart—a hot-rod golf cart. The driver weaved his way in and out of lanes with complete disregard for pedestrians and traffic signals.

Philip took her by the hand and led her through the lobby, around the huge swimming pool in back of the hotel and to the stairs that descended to the beach. The strip of white sand stretched as far as the eye could see. So did the array of hotels.

"I don't suppose you've been in the ocean yet."

"No time," Carla confessed. "The first thing Nancy and I did was take a shower." The heat that had greeted them on their arrival had been suffocating. They'd stepped from the air-conditioned plane into one-hundred-degree weather. By the time they'd arrived at the hotel room, their clothes had been damp and clinging. "I couldn't believe that death trap of a shuttle bus actually made it all the way to the hotel."

Philip grinned in amusement. "I think the same thing every time I visit."

"Do you come often?" Carla asked as they sat in the sand and removed their shoes. Philip rolled up the tan pant legs to his knees.

"Once or twice a year."

He stood and tucked her hand into the crook of his arm.

"I think there's something I should tell you," Carla said as an ocean wave gently lapped up to her bare feet. The warm water was another surprise.

"You mean that you don't usually pick up men in bars," Philip said with a chuckle. "I already knew that."

"You did?" Carla was astonished.

"What made you do it this time?"

Carla kicked idly at the sand with her big toe. "You aren't going to like this," she mumbled.

"Try me."

She took a deep breath, then exhaled slowly. "It happens every vacation. Nancy and I spend the entire time waiting to meet someone. This time we decided that instead of wasting our vacation, we'd simply settle for someone we could find on the first day. You came in alone. You're under thirty-five. You ordered a margarita."

The pleasant sound of his laughter blended with a crashing wave that pounded the beach. "I almost asked for a beer."

"I'm glad you didn't." The words were automatic and sincere. It surprised Carla how much she meant them.

The sun became a huge red ball that slowly descended to meet a blue horizon. Carla couldn't remember ever seeing anything more spectacular. She glanced at Philip to see if he was also enjoying the beauty of their surroundings. He wasn't the chatty sort, she realized, which was fine—she could do enough talking for both of them. His laugh was free and easy, and the sound of it warmed her.

"What were you reading so intently on the plane?" Carla asked, curious to know more about him.

"The latest book by Ann Rule, she's—"

"I know who she is," Carla interrupted. The talented Seattle author was a policewoman turned reporter turned writer. Ann's books specialized in crime. Her novel on serial murderer Ted Bundy was a national best-seller. "My father worked with Ann before she took up writing," Carla explained. "She's from Seattle."

"I read that on the cover flap. What does your father do?"

Carla swallowed uncomfortably. "He's a cop," she murmured, not looking at Philip.

"You sound like it bothers you."

"It does," Carla replied vigorously. "Half the boys in high school wouldn't ask me out. They were afraid I'd tell my father if they tried anything, and then he'd go after them."

"Your father would arrest them for making a pass?" Philip sounded incredulous.

"Not that." She tossed him a defiant glare. It was obvious that Philip, like everyone else in her life, didn't understand. "It's too hard to explain."

"Try."

Carla felt a tightening in her stomach. Although she'd held these feelings deep inside since childhood, she had never verbalized them. She didn't know how to express them now. "A good example of what I'm saying happened when I was about ten. Our family went to my friend's wedding reception. Everyone had been drinking, and an uncle had given some of the teens spiked punch. The minute Dad walked in the room the temperature dropped fifteen degrees."

"Were they afraid he was going to make a scene?"

"I don't know. But I do recall how uncomfortable everyone was."

"Including you?"

She hesitated. "Yes."

"But that's not all, is it?" he asked gently.

"No," she admitted. "It was far more than that. I can count on one hand the number of Christmases Dad spent home. It was the same thing every holiday. And we were lucky if he was there for our birthdays. It got so that I'd dread it every time the phone rang, because I knew he was always on call. It was his job."

"I don't blame you for resenting that."

Once started, Carla discovered she couldn't stop. "He worked with the scum of the earth: pimps, prostitutes, muggers, murderers, drunks and derelicts. Then there were the sick people, dying people, dead people, wife beaters and child abusers. Sometimes he'd come home at night and..." She stopped, realizing that everything had come out in one huge rush. When she'd caught her breath, Carla continued. "I'm sorry, I didn't mean to do this to you."

"You didn't," Philip said, and casually draped his hand over her shoulder. "You've never told your father any of this, have you?"

"No. What was the use? Dad loves his work." Philip's hand cupped her shoulder. He was comforting her, and in a strange way Carla appreciated it. Never before had she voiced these thoughts, and the fierce intensity of her feelings had surprised her.

By unspoken mutual agreement, they turned back toward the hotel. The sky had grown dark now, and the lights from the long row of hotels dimly lit the beach. Other couples were walking along the sandy shores. A few flirted with the cresting ocean waves.

"Philip." Carla stopped and turned toward him. "Thank you," she whispered.

"What for?"

Their eyes met in the moonlight, and Carla was trapped in the silvery glow of his gaze. Those beautiful, warm gray eyes held her as effectively as the arms that had slipped around her waist and brought her into his embrace.

"I may never drink anything but margaritas again." His whisper was husky, but he didn't make a move to do anything more than hold her. His arms pressed her gently, undemandingly, as he rubbed his chin across the top of her head. A mist-filled breeze off the ocean had ruined her carefully styled hair; now it fell in tight ringlets around her oval face.

Her hair was another thing that endeared her to Philip. Not once had he mentioned its color. Men invariably teased her about it, asking if her temper matched the color of her hair. The only time it did was when someone made tiresome remarks about it. Not red and not blond, the shade fell somewhere in between. Red oak, her mother claimed, like her grandmother's. Like russet potatoes, her brother suggested. The color of her hair and her fair complexion had been the bane of Carla's existence.

"Would you like to go for a swim?" Philip asked, dropping his arms and taking her hand. They continued walking toward the hotel.

"In the ocean?" She'd have to get her suit.

"No, the current's too dangerous. I meant the pool."

The hotel's swimming pool was the most luxurious Carla had ever seen. A picture of the massive pool area at the hotel had been the determining factor in their decision to book their holidays at the El Cid. Blue, watery channels stretched all around the hotel, with bridges joining one section to another.

"I'd love to go swimming," Carla replied enthusiastically. They reached the short flight of stairs that led to the hotel from the beach. "Give me ten minutes to change and I'll meet you back here."

"Ten minutes?" Philip arched one brow. Carla had noticed him do that a couple of times during the evening. It seemed to be Philip's way of expressing mild surprise.

"Ten minutes—easy," Carla confirmed confidently. She knew exactly which corner of her suitcase held her swimsuit. It wouldn't take her more than five minutes to change, so she figured she'd easily have five minutes to spare. But what she hadn't counted on was that Nancy had neatly stored their suitcases under the beds. Carla spent a frantic five minutes tearing their room apart, certain that they'd been robbed. Finally, she found it. She should have remembered her friend's penchant for neatness.

Fifteen minutes later, a chagrined look pinching her face, Carla met Philip at poolside.

Pointedly he glanced at his watch.

"I couldn't help it," she told him breathlessly, and offered a sketchy explanation as she placed her towel on a chaise longue. The pool was empty, which surprised Carla until she removed her gold wristwatch and noted that it was after midnight.

She tugged the elastic of the forest-green maillot over her thigh and tested the water by dipping one foot into the pool. Warm. Almost too warm.

"Are you one of those women who gets wet by degrees?" Philip asked as he took off his glasses and tossed them on his towel.

"Not me." She walked to his side, stretched out her arms and dived in. Her slim body sliced into the water. Philip joined her almost immediately, and together they swam the width of the pool.

"Do you want to race?" he called out.

"No," Carla answered with a giggle.

"Why not?"

"Because I was on my college swim team, and I'm fast. Men can't stand to lose."

"Is that a fact?"

"It's true."

"I'm not like most men."

Carla had noticed that. But this was turning out to be a promising relationship, and she didn't want to ruin it. Floating lackadaisically on her back, she paddled rhythmically with her hands at her side. Carla decided to ignore the challenge in his voice.

Philip joined her, floating on his back as well. "If you don't want to race, what would you like to do?"

"Kiss underwater." She laughed at the shocked look on his face as he struggled to a standing position. Philip looked different without his glasses, almost handsome. But not quite.

He stood completely still in the shoulder-deep water. "I'm not that kind of man."

He was so serious that it took Carla a moment to realize he was kidding.

"I'm not easy, you know," she said, flirting. "You have to catch me first." They were acting like adolescents, and Carla loved it. With Philip she could be herself. There wasn't any need to put on sophisticated airs.

Laughing, she twisted and dived underwater, surfacing several feet away from him. He came after her, and Carla took off with all the energy she'd expend for an important race. Using her most powerful strokes, she surged ahead. When his hand groped for her foot, she kicked frantically and managed to escape. That he'd caught up with her so quickly was hard to believe.

She was even more amazed when his solid stroke matched hers and he gripped her waist and pulled her to the side of the pool.

"Damn, you're as slippery as an eel."

"Damn, you're good," she countered. "Who taught you to swim like that?"

"My mother." They were hidden under the shadow of a bridge that crossed a narrow section of the pool.

Carla slipped her arms around his neck. She wanted him to kiss her. Philip was probably the kind of man who figured he had to see a girl two or three times before he'd try anything. But he was attracted to her; she'd seen it in his eyes when they were on the beach. That look had prompted her flippant challenge about kissing underwater.

He pushed the wet strands of hair from her face. The silver light in his eyes darkened dramatically. He moved closer, but Carla assumed it was because he couldn't see her clearly without his glasses. She liked his eyes. They were so expressive. She liked the way they darkened when he was serious and how they sparkled when he was teasing. Tiny lines fanned out from the edges, and Carla recognized that this man laughed and enjoyed life. Her feelings for him were intensifying every minute they were together.

His hand rested on either side of her face, pressing her against the side of the pool. "I'm going to kiss you," he whispered. He released one hand and encircled her waist to pull her gently but firmly toward him.

Slowly, lengthening each moment, each breath, he lowered his mouth to hers. Carla felt herself relax, felt her body, her heart, opening to him. Wanting to touch him, needing to, she ran her hand along the side of his face, twisting her head so that when he found her lips their mouths slanted across each other's. The kiss was gentle and soft, gradually building in intensity until Carla melted against him.

Philip let go of the side of the pool, and they sank just below the surface. Their legs entwined, and Carla opened her mouth to him. His tongue sought hers, forcing her mouth to open farther under its exploring pressure. Carla felt as if she were drowning, but the sensation was exquisite.

They broke the surface of the water together and drew in deep, shaky breaths. Her body remained tucked in his embrace. His chest pressed against the softness of her breasts, and a crazy dizziness overcame her.

The pressure of his embrace backed her against the side of the pool, and he kissed her again. Carla gloried in the wonderful, inexplicable sensations that overwhelmed her.

Their breathing was ragged when Philip buried his face in the side of her neck.

"My word," she murmured breathlessly, "who taught you to kiss like that?"

Philip responded with a weak laugh. "Not my mother."

"I should hope not."

"Carla." Philip hesitated and wiped the moisture from his eyes. "Damn, I wish I could see you better."

"I'm glad you can't," she replied happily. "You might get a swelled head if you could see how much I like you."

"Carla." His voice grew strong, serious.

"What's wrong?" She placed a hand on each of his shoulders, liking the feel of her body floating against his.

"There's something you should know."

"What?" He was so serious that her heart throbbed. She didn't want anything to ruin this.

"Carla, I'm a policeman for the city of Spokane."

Chapter Two

Carla woke just as the sun crested the horizon and bathed the beach in a flashy glow of color. Nancy had been asleep by the time Carla had returned last night, which was just as well. She hadn't felt much like talking.

Philip Garrison had taught her a valuable lesson. She should have trusted her instincts. From her first look at Philip, she'd felt he wasn't her type. At the time, she hadn't realized how true that was. True, his kisses had been... She couldn't find a word to describe them. Pleasant, she mused. All right, very pleasant. But that certainly wasn't enough to overcome *what* he was.

Damn, damn, damn. She'd liked him. She'd liked him a lot. He was sensitive, sympathetic, compassionate, kind, caring... Carla placed the pillow over her head to drown out her thoughts. She wouldn't allow herself to think about him again. This crazy idea of Nancy's had been ridiculous from the beginning. She'd put the episode behind her and get on with her vacation.

Throwing back the covers of her bed, she stood and stretched. Nancy grumbled and curled into a tight ball. Typical of Nancy, who hated mornings.

"What time is it?" she demanded in a growling whisper.

"Early, the sun just came up."

"Sun!" Nancy's eyes popped open. "I forgot to set the alarm."

Carla smiled as she sat in the middle of the single bed and ran a brush through her hair to tame the wild array of red curls. "Don't worry about the time. We're on vacation, remember?"

With an uncharacteristically hurried movement, Nancy threw back the sheets. "But I promised to meet Eduardo on the beach at dawn," she cried out. "Oh, good grief, how could I have been so stupid?"

For Nancy to forget anything was surprising by itself. But to have her friend show this much enthusiasm in the morning was astonishing.

"I take it you and...Eduardo hit it off?" Carla had almost called him Mr. Chips.

Nancy's head bobbed energetically. "What about you?"

"Not so lucky," Carla returned with a wistful sigh.

Nancy's most attractive summer dress slid over her hips as she turned her back to Carla in an unspoken request for her to do up the zipper. "What went wrong?"

"You don't have time to hear," Carla said with forced cheerfulness.

"He looked nice."

Nice was only the beginning, Carla thought. "Looks are often deceiving." That much was true. Who would have imagined that Philip Garrison would turn out to be so appealing? "If I'm not mistaken, I'd say you and Eduardo got along famously."

"He's fabulous. I can't remember a night I've enjoyed more." Nancy paused, and a dreamy look replaced the hurried frown that had marred her smooth features.

"His cast doesn't bother you?" Carla couldn't help asking.

"Good grief, no. I hardly thought about it."

That was saying something.

"He's taking me on an all-day tour of Mazatlán. You don't mind, do you?"

"Mind? Me? Of course not." Carla's mouth formed a tight smile. Now she'd be forced to spend the entire day alone. "Have a good time," she managed without a hint of sarcasm. No need to ruin Nancy's fun.

"Thanks, I will." Always practical, Nancy grabbed a hat to protect her from the sun, tucked her travelers' checks in a secret flap in her purse and was out the door in a rush.

Carla flopped back on her bed and stared at the shadows on the ceiling. This vacation was rapidly turning into a disaster. Day two and already she wished she were back in Seattle.

After an unhurried shower, Carla decided to head for the pool. With her skin color, she wasn't able to stay out long, and morning was generally the best time for her to sunbathe.

The pool area was filling up with early sun worshippers, and Carla chose a chaise longue near the deep end. That way she could dive in and cool off whenever necessary. This afternoon she'd do some shopping at the Mazatlán Arts and Crafts Center. She'd heard about the center almost immediately after her arrival. With twenty-eight shops to explore, she was certain to find souvenirs for her family. But even shopping had lost its appeal, especially since she'd be doing it alone. If she was lucky, she might meet someone at the pool—preferably someone male and handsome. Rich wouldn't hurt, either.

She spread her towel out as a cushion for the longue and lay on her stomach, facing the pool. With her arms crossed she pressed her cheeks against her forearm. Boring, she admitted regretfully. Day two and she was bored to death. The turquoise bikini she wore was modest, especially when compared to the daring suit on the luscious, curvy creature across the pool from her. Carla guessed that if she had a body like that, she might be tempted to wear the same thing. She'd heard of string bikinis, but this one was hardly more than threads. The woman was attracting the attention of almost everyone at poolside. When Philip moved into her line of vision, Carla's eyes widened. He smiled, and his gray eyes twinkled. It didn't bother her that his smile wasn't directed at her. For all the attention he'd given her, he obviously hadn't noticed that she was across the pool from him.

Carla chose to ignore him, but her heart leaped at the sight he made. He wasn't muscular or strikingly masculine, but he was compelling in a way she couldn't describe. If she hadn't spent yesterday with him, she wouldn't have given him a second look today. But she'd felt the lean hardness of him against her in the water. She'd tasted the sweetness of his kiss. She'd experienced the gentle comfort of his arms. Her eyes refused to move from him, and when he looked her way, she shook herself from her musings and lowered her cheek against her arm, pretending not to see him.

Her heart was racing and that angered her. One look from Philip was no reason for her pulse to quicken. Although Carla refused to pay attention to him, she could feel Philip's gaze on her. A smile played upon her lips as she imagined the satisfaction in his gaze, the look of admiration that would dominate those smoky-gray eyes of his. How she loved those expressive eyes of his! Unable to resist, she raised her head a fraction to catch a glimpse of his approval. To her dismay, Carla discovered that Philip wasn't studying her at all. His concentration was centered on the daring blond beauty at the other side of the pool.

Carla expected the woman to treat Philip like a pesky intruder. But she didn't—in fact, she seemed to encourage his attentions. Grudgingly, Carla admitted there *was* a kind of lithe attraction to Philip, and an aura of quiet confidence that was . . . well, masculine. His sandy hair had a tendency to curl at the ends, she observed, and most men would have styled it into submission. But not Philip; professionally groomed hair wouldn't be on his list of priorities.

After several minutes of what appeared to be light conversation, Philip dived into the pool and did a number of laps. Carla couldn't help admiring the way his bronze body sliced through the water. Anyone would. A rush of pink colored her cheeks as she recalled their antics last night. Yes, Philip Garrison was indeed gifted.

When Philip came out of the pool, he maneuvered himself so that he "accidentally" dripped water on his scantily clad acquaintance. The luscious blonde sat up to hand him a towel and laughed lightly when more drops of water splashed on her bare midriff.

Forcefully, Carla directed her gaze elsewhere. For a full five minutes she refused to allow herself to turn their way. When curiosity got the better of her, Carla casually returned her attention to the couple, who were an unlikely match. They were laughing and enjoying a cocktail. One side of Carla's mouth curved up sarcastically. One would assume a dedicated police officer would know better than to consume alcohol at such an early hour.

Pretending that the sun was burning her tender skin, Carla made a show of standing and draping a light terry-cloth wrap over her shoulders. She tucked her towel and tanning lotion in the oversized bag and walked down the cement stairs that led to the beach.

The beach wasn't nearly as crowded as the pool area. Carla had just settled in the sandy mattress when she was approached by a vendor carrying a black case. He knelt in front of her and opened the lid to display a large number of silver earrings, bracelets and rings. She smiled and shook her head. But the man persisted, telling her in poor English that he would sell jewelry to her at a very good price.

Politely but firmly, Carla shook her head.

Still the man insisted, holding out a lovely silver-and-turquoise ring for her to inspect. His eyes pleaded with her, and Carla couldn't refuse. The ring was pretty.

Someone spoke in Spanish from behind her. It didn't take Carla two seconds to realize it was Philip. His words were heavy with authority, although he hadn't raised his voice. Resenting his intrusion, she tossed him an angry look.

"Do you like the ring?" He directed his comment to her.

"Well, it's more than I wanted to spend—"

She wasn't allowed to finish. Philip said something to the vendor, who nodded resignedly, took back the ring and turned away.

"That wasn't necessary, you know," she told him stiffly.

"Perhaps not, but you could buy the same ring in the hotel gift shop for less than what he was asking." Philip spread out his towel a respectable distance from her. "Do you mind?" he asked before he sat down.

"It's a public beach," she returned coolly, recognizing it wouldn't do any good to object. "Just leave enough space between us so no one will assume we're together." Philip would only follow her if she got up and moved. "What happened with Miss String Bikini?'' Carla had hoped to resist any hint of acid in her query.

Philip chuckled. "Unfortunately, Miss is a Mrs., and hubby looked like the jealous type."

Now it was Carla's turn to laugh. She was sorry to have missed the scene of Philip meeting the irate husband. "I'll admit, though, she had quite a body."

"Passable," Philip admitted dryly as his eyes swept over the beach.

Passable! Carla's mind echoed, wondering what he considered terrific.

"Where's your roommate?" he asked breezily.

"With...Eduardo. They seem to have hit it off quite well."

"We did, too, as I recall. I wonder what it would take to get you to agree to have lunch with me."

"Forget it, Garrison," Carla said forcefully.

"You know what a good time we could have," he prodded softly.

"I'm not interested," Carla replied without looking at him. She felt a twinge of regret at how callous she sounded, and recalled how cold she'd been to him after he'd told her about himself. She wouldn't have been so unfeeling, she suspected, if she hadn't previously expressed her resentment about her father being a policeman. Later, unable to sleep, she decided she was glad she'd told him. It had saved an unnecessary explanation. As it was, she'd pushed herself from his arms and swum to the opposite side of the pool. "It was a pleasure meeting you, Philip Garrison," she'd said tersely while toweling dry. "But I have one strict code regarding the men I date."

"I think I can guess what that is," he'd replied with a control that was frightening. "You realize I didn't have to tell you. We could have had a pleasant vacation together without your ever being the wiser."

"Perhaps." Carla hadn't been in any mood to reason. "But you saved us both a lot of trouble." With the damp towel draped over her neck, she'd practically run to her room. Not until she'd changed out of her swimsuit had Carla realized how miserable she was. Disappointed in herself and disappointed in Philip. He might as well have admitted to being married; he was as off limits as if he had a wife and ten children.

"Nice-looking brunette to your left," Philip pointed out, breaking her train of thought.

"It doesn't look like she's sporting a jealous husband, either," Carla said jokingly.

Philip's laugh was good-natured. "I'll use my practised routine on her. Care to watch me in action?"

"I'd love it," Carla answered with open delight. "At least with you out of the picture some handsome tourist can make a play for me."

"Good luck," he called as he stood and loped lazily down the beach.

Handsome tourist; Carla almost laughed. At the rate things were going, the only men she'd be fighting off would be persistent vendors.

Carla watched with growing interest as Philip carelessly tossed his towel on the beach close to the girl and ran into the rolling surf. She'd remember to ask him later about swimming in the ocean. Last night he'd told her the tide was too dangerous, yet he was diving headlong into it without a second's hesitation.

After a few minutes, which he apparently thought suitable for a favorable impression, he stood, wiped the water from his face and walked out of the ocean. He squinted and rubbed his eyes, giving the impression the water was stinging. The way he groped for his towel made Carla laugh outright. Again by an apparent accident, he flicked sand on the tanning beauty. The girl sat up and brushed the offending particles from her well-oiled body. Philip fell to his knees, and although Carla couldn't hear what he was saying, she was sure it was some practised apology. Soon the two of them were talking and laughing. Spreading out his long body, he lay beside the brown-haired beauty. His technique, tried and true, had worked well. Rolling his head, Philip caught Carla's gaze and smiled when she gestured with two fingers, giving the okay sign.

For the first time in recent memory, Carla wished that she were as good at acting as Philip. For a moment she toyed with the idea of following his lead and blatantly approaching a man. Carla's devil-may-care system should work as well on the beach as in the cocktail lounge. But a quick survey of the area didn't turn up a single male she cared to flirt with. There wasn't anyone she particularly wanted to meet. Maybe Nancy was right, maybe she had become much too picky lately.

Ten minutes later, Carla stood, brushed the sand from her skin and picked up her things. After lunch she'd do some shopping.

Philip gave her a brief wave, which she returned. At least one of them had been successful. At least one of them was having a good time.

The oppressive afternoon heat eventually brought Carla back into the air-conditioned cocktail lounge. Sipping a pina colada, she surveyed the growing crowd of tourists. A couple of times men had asked if they could buy her a drink, but she'd declined. Men who used tanning machines, wore gold chains around their necks and left their shirts open to their navels didn't interest Carla. Her spirits were low, and she hated to think she'd be fighting this depression the entire week. If she wasn't careful, she'd get locked in a state of self-pity.

The room was filling up rapidly, and when Philip entered Carla pretended an inordinate amount of interest in her drink.

"Hi." He sauntered to her side. "Do you mind if I join you, or will I be distracting any potential margarita drinkers?"

"By all means join me," she said with a poor attempt at a smile. "I don't exactly seem to be drawing a crowd. How about you? I expected you to stroll in here with Miss September."

He cleared his throat and took the plush seat beside her. "That didn't work out."

"Was there a Mr. September?"

"No." Philip cleared his throat a second time. "Things didn't work out, that's all."

"Philip," she moaned impatiently, "come on, tell me what happened. You can't leave me in suspense like this." Something perverse inside her wanted to know

about Philip's latest rejection. Maybe she needed to
salve her pride at his expense, which was childish,
Carla thought, but shared misery beats the solo kind.

He ignored her while he raised his hand to attract
the waitress's attention. "What's that you're drinking?"

"Pina colada," Carla answered quickly. "Out with
it, Garrison. Details, I want details."

The waitress came to take his order. Carla had lost
the desire to impress him with her vast knowledge of
the Spanish language. As it was, the waitress eyed her
warily, as if she were afraid Carla were a loco gringo.

"No margarita tonight?" His eyes mocked hers as
a smile touched the corners of his mouth.

"Don't change the subject."

"I'll tell you over dinner." He raised both thick
brows suggestively.

"Do you think bribing me is going to work?"

He smiled faintly, rather tenderly, at her. "I was
hoping it would."

This was the best offer she'd had all day. And she
wasn't about to refuse. "All right, as long as we understand one another."

"Of course we do," he replied formally. "You don't
want to date cops, and with good reason."

"With damn good reason," she repeated emphati-
cally.

The waitress delivered their drinks and brought a
plate with two tacos, or what Carla assumed were tacos. She'd noticed that a sign outside the lounge stated
that anyone buying a drink between four and five
would receive a free taco. But this fried corn tortilla

that had been filled with meat and rolled didn't resemble anything she'd call a taco. No lettuce, no cheese, no tomato.

One nibble confirmed that it didn't taste anything like one, either. "What's in this?"

Philip eyed her doubtfully. "Are you sure you want to know?"

"Of course I do."

He shrugged. "Turtle."

Carla closed her eyes and swallowed. "Turtle," she repeated. "It tastes more like week-old tuna fish to me."

"You don't have to eat it if you don't want."

She set it back on the plate. "It's something to tell my friends about, but it's nothing I'd recommend."

"It'll grow on you," Philip commented.

"I certainly hope not," Carla said with a grimace. "Have you ever examined the skin on those things?"

Suddenly they were both laughing as if she'd said the most uproariously funny thing in the world. "Come on." His hand reached for hers. "Let's get out of here before they throw us out." He laid several bills beside their uneaten turtle tacos. Together, hand in hand, they practically ran out of the cocktail lounge.

Not until they were in a golf cart/taxi did Carla ask where they were headed.

"Senor Frog's," Philip shouted, the wind whipping his voice past her.

"No." She waved her hand dramatically. "Not if they serve what I think they do."

"Not to worry." Philip placed an arm around her shoulder and spoke close to her ear. "This is a famous tourist trap. The food's good, but the place is wild. You'll love it.''

And just as he'd promised, Carla did love it. After almost an hour's delay, they were ushered through the restaurant doors only to be led to a cocktail lounge. The music and boisterous singing were so loud that Carla couldn't hear herself speak when she leaned over to ask Philip something. He bent closer but finally gestured that they'd have to talk afterward outside.

Two hours later, well fed and singing softly, Carla and Philip left the restaurant with their arms wrapped around each other.

"That was wild."

"I knew you'd like it," Philip said, smiling tenderly at her.

"But there's a method to your madness."

"How's that?"

"With all the noise, you weren't able to tell me about Miss September."

"All right, if you must know."

"I must," she replied firmly. "I hope you realize I baked in the hot sun while I waited to see how you did. Honestly, Philip, your approach could have been a little more original."

The look he gave told her that he was offended. "I thought my technique was one of a kind."

Carla looked at the darkening sky and rolled her eyes, but refrained from comment. "I'm surprised that you didn't go up to her and ask if you'd met someplace before."

Philip shifted his weight onto the other foot. "To be honest, that occurred to me, too."

Laughing, Carla slipped her arm through his. "You, my dear Philip, are refreshingly unimaginative."

He made a funny little noise that sounded as if he were clearing his throat. He seemed to be studying the cracks in the sidewalk on which they were strolling. He didn't appear to have any clear direction.

"Now, will you spill the beans about Miss September? I'm dying to know what happened."

He was quiet for a few moments. "You prefer not to date policemen, and I have a thing about stewardesses."

Most men had a "thing" about stewardesses, too, but it wasn't to avoid them. It wasn't one of her more brilliant deductions to guess that Philip had once loved a stewardess and been hurt. "Do you want to tell me about her? I make a great wailing wall," she murmured sympathetically.

"Not if I can avoid it." He looked at her and smiled. "Tell me about your afternoon. Any success?"

"No one," she said dejectedly, and shook her head for emphasis. "Unless you count guys in gold chains who enjoy revealing their chest hair."

"Some women like those kind of men."

"Not me."

Philip hesitated, then asked, "I wonder if I could interest you in a short-term, no-obligation, strictly regulated, but guaranteed fun relationship."

Carla's mouth curved wryly. She'd had a better time with Philip tonight than the entire day she'd spent alone. Her mind was flashing a bright neon "NO" in bold red letters. If she had any sense whatsoever, she'd shake her head and decline without another word.

"Well?" he urged.

"I don't know," she answered truthfully. Five days, what could possibly happen in five days? She'd come to Mexico looking for a good time. She knew who Philip was and, more important, *what* he was.

The silence lengthened. "I think I should make one thing clear. I have no intention of treating you like a sister."

He could have lied. But again, he'd chosen to be straight with her. She appreciated that.

"I don't want anything more than these five days. Once we leave Mazatlán it's over."

"Agreed," he said, and a finger tenderly traced the outline of her delicate jaw.

A tingling sensation burned across her face, and she closed her eyes against its potency. She'd be safe. She'd walked into this with her eyes wide open. He lived in Spokane. She lived in Seattle. A light flirtation was what she'd had in mind in the first place. Knowing what he was should make it all the easier to walk away next Saturday. But it hadn't lessened the attraction she felt for him—and that appeared to be growing every minute.

"I...haven't agreed yet." Her pride demanded one last stand.

"But you will," Philip said confidently.

"How can you be so sure?" Carla returned, piqued by his attitude.

"Well, for one thing, you're looking at me with 'kiss me' eyes."

Embarrassed, Carla shot her gaze to the ground. "That's not true," she denied hotly, and was ready to argue further, but Philip cut her off.

"Do you agree or not?" He held out his hand for her to shake.

"I have a feeling I'm going to regret this," she said, and placed her hand in his.

Philip didn't argue. But when his arm closed around her shoulders, she didn't object. She liked the idea of being linked with this man, even if it was only for a few days.

"How about a ride on an araña?" he suggested, his mouth disturbingly close to her ear.

"I don't know what you're suggesting, Philip Garrison, but that doesn't sound like something nice girls do."

His laughter filled the night. "That's a two-wheeled, horse-drawn cab."

"Sounds romantic." Knowing Philip, Carla was willing to bet he'd instruct the driver to take the long way back to the hotel through scented, shady boulevards. She was in the mood for a few stolen kisses, and so was Philip, gauging by his look.

"If we can't find one, we can always jog back to the hotel," he said seriously.

"With a name like Walker you expect me to run?"

"What's the matter with running? I thought you'd be into physical fitness."

She laughed softly. "I swim, and that's the entire repertoire of my athletic abilities."

"You mean you weren't in track? With those long legs of yours, I'd think you'd be a natural."

"So did my high school coach—until the first practice. He had to time me with a calendar. Running's out."

"Walking?" Philip suggested.

"Good grief, if we can't find a carriage, what's the matter with those golf-cart things that we've been taking lately?"

"You mean the pulmonias?" His gray eyes were dancing with amusement, and Carla struggled not to succumb to the invitation in their smoky depths.

"Whatever," she replied, pleased with herself now for agreeing to this crazy relationship. She honestly enjoyed this zany man.

"If you insist," Philip said blandly, and flagged down a passing taxi when it became obvious that finding an araña would take longer than they were willing to wait.

Back at the hotel Carla mentally chastised herself for being so easily swayed by Philip's direct approach. She really ought to have played harder to get.

"There's a band playing at the—"

"I love to dance," she interrupted enthusiastically. "My feet are itching already."

Philip smoothed the hair at the side of his head. "Tell me, why was I expecting an argument?" He was regarding her with a look of amused surprise.

"I don't know." Carla laughed gaily, happiness bubbling over.

"If you're not into sports, what kinds of things do you like to do?" With his hand at her elbow, he escorted her toward the lively sounds of the mariachi band.

"Play checkers," Carla responded immediately. "I've won the King County Park and Recreational checker championship three years running. It's a nice friendly game, and I've got a terrific coach I'll tell you about sometime."

Carla felt relaxed and happy as they stood in line outside the lounge. They seemed to be waiting in a lot of lines tonight, not that she minded.

Philip was studying her intently; his eyes narrowed slightly as if he had trouble assimilating the fact she was nonathletic.

"No sports, you say?"

"Just checkers." Carla's gleaming eyes didn't leave his. "Knowing that I'm a champion, Philip, would you have any trouble jumping me?" She was teasing, but the responding look in Philip's eyes was serious.

"I'd consider it," he murmured, "but I think I'd probably wait until after the game."

Chapter Three

Golden moonbeams softly lighted a path along the beach. The gentle whisper of the ocean breeze was broken only by the sound of the waves crashing against the smooth white shore.

Philip slipped his arm around Carla's shoulders, and she brought her hand up so that they could lace their fingers together.

"Why didn't you tell me you could dance like that?" he murmured against her hair. "I've seen card sharks with slower moves."

Enjoying his surprise, Carla smiled softly to herself. "All I do is swing my hips a little."

"Yes, but I felt the least I could do was try to keep up with you. I'm dead."

"And I thought you cops had to be in top physical condition." Not for a minute would she admit that she was as exhausted as Philip.

"I'm in great shape," he argued, "but three hours on the dance floor with you is above and beyond the call of duty. Next time I think I'll suggest checkers."

"You'll lose," Carla returned confidently.

"Maybe, but I have a feeling my feet won't hurt nearly as much."

Philip had been the one to suggest this stroll. But it wasn't a walk in the moonlight that interested him; Carla was convinced of that. He was seeking a few stolen kisses against the backdrop of a tropical night. And for that matter, so was she. Every time they met, Philip astonished her. One look the day on the plane and she'd instantly sized him up as dull and introspective. But he was warm, caring and witty. There wasn't any man who could make her laugh the way Philip did.

"I enjoyed myself tonight. You're a lot of fun." She felt compelled to tell him that.

"You sound surprised." Philip moved his chin so it brushed against the crown of her head. The action was strangely comforting and almost erotic.

"Surprised is the wrong word," she said softly, struggling to express herself. "Leery, maybe. I don't want to like you too much. That would only complicate a nice, serene relationship. We're having a good time, and I don't want to ruin it."

"In other words, you don't want to fall in love with me?"

"Exactly." Carla hated the heartless way this made her sound. Already she recognized that falling for Philip wouldn't be difficult. He was many of the things she wanted in a man. And everything she didn't.

He expelled his breath in a half-angry sigh, but it was the only indication he gave that she had displeased him.

Closing her eyes, Carla felt an unexpected rush of regret settle over her. One evening together and she was already doubting that this arrangement was going to work. Spending time with Philip might not be a good idea if they were both going to end up taking it seriously. All she wanted was a good time. And he'd claimed that was all he was looking for. This was a holiday fling, after all, not a husband hunt.

"Don't you think you're overreacting just a little to the fact I'm a policeman?" Philip asked, his voice restrained and searching.

"Haven't we already been over this?" she answered hastily. "Besides, you have your own dating quirk. What if I'd been a flight attendant? You said yourself you prefer not to go out with them."

"But in your case I'd have made an exception."

"Why?"

"It's those lovely eyes of yours—"

"No," she interrupted brusquely, reacting with more than simple curiosity. "Why don't you like stewardesses?"

"It's a long story, and there are other things I have in mind." Clearly he wasn't interested in relating the details of his experience, and Carla decided she wouldn't push him. When he was ready to tell her, if he ever was, she'd be pleased to listen. She found it interesting that after only a few hours' acquaintance with Philip she had released a lifetime full of bitterness about her father and his occupation. Apparently, she hadn't generated the same kind of response in him. It troubled her a little.

"You're quiet all of a sudden." His lips found her temple, and he kissed her there lightly. "What are you thinking?"

Tilting her head back, she smiled into those appealing smoky-gray eyes of his. "To be honest, I was mulling over the fact that you'll tell me about your hang-ups in time. But then it occurred to me that you might not."

"And that bothers you?" He studied her with amused patience.

"Yes and no." In a way that she didn't understand, Carla suddenly decided she didn't want to know. Obviously Philip had loved and presumably lost, and Carla wasn't sure she wanted the particulars.

"The curious side of you is eager to hear the gory details—"

"But my sensitive side doesn't want to have you dredge up unhappy memories," she finished for him.

"It was a long time ago."

Carla slipped an arm around his waist and laid her head against his shoulder. "And best forgotten."

They continued walking along the moonlit beach in silence. Carla felt warm and comfortable having this man at her side. The realization wasn't something she wanted to explore; for now she was content.

"It's been six years since I broke up with Nicole," Philip said after a time.

Twisting in his embrace, Carla turned and pressed the tips of her fingers against his lips. "Don't," she whispered, afraid how she'd react if she saw pain in his eyes. "It isn't necessary. There isn't a reason in the world for you to tell me."

His jaw tightened, and memories played across his expressive face. Some revealed the pleasant aspects of his relationship with Nicole, but others weren't as easily deciphered.

"I think you should know," he said, and his eyes narrowed to hard points of steel.

Carla wasn't sure which was troubling him more: the past or the sudden need to tell her about Nicole.

"Let me simplify things by saying that I loved her and asked her to marry me. But apparently she didn't care as deeply for me as I thought."

"She turned you down?" Carla murmured.

"No." His short laugh was filled with bitter sarcasm. "That's the crazy part. Nicole accepted my ring, but she refused to move out on the guy she was living with."

Carla struggled not to laugh. "If you want my opinion, I think you made a lucky escape. This Nicole sounds a bit kinky to me."

Philip relaxed against her. His hands found the small of her back, arching her closer to him. "I don't know, there's something about me that attracts the weird ones. Just yesterday some oddball approached me in the bar with a lunatic story about me being her date for the night because I ordered a margarita."

"A real weirdo, no doubt." One brow arched mockingly.

"That's not the half of it." His head lowered with every word, so that by the time he finished, his lips hovered over hers.

"Oh?" Breathlessly she anticipated his kiss.

"Yes." His low voice was as caressing as his look. "The thing is, I'd been watching her from the moment I walked into the lounge, trying to come up with a way of approaching her."

Before she could react to this startling bit of news, Philip brought her into his embrace. Slowly his mouth opened over hers, taking in the softness of her trembling lips in a soul-stirring, devouring kiss. Carla stood on the tips of her toes and clung to him, devastated by the intensity of her reaction. This had happened the first time he'd kissed her. If Philip's lovemaking had been hard or urgent, maybe she could have withstood it. But he was incredibly gentle, as if she were of exquisite worth and as fragile as a rosebud, and that was irresistible.

When his tongue outlined the fullness of her mouth, Carla's willpower melted, and she couldn't pull herself away from the fiery kiss. Flames of passion shot through her, and when she broke away, her breathing was irregular and deep.

"I . . . I think we should put a limit on those," she proposed shakily.

Philip didn't look any more in control of himself than she felt. His eyes were closed as he drew in a husky breath and nodded in agreement. Only a short space separated them, but he continued to hold her, his hands running the length of her bare arms.

"Let's get you back to your hotel room."

"Yes."

But they didn't move.

Unable to resist, Carla rested her head against his muscular chest, weak with the wonder of his kiss. "I just don't understand." She was surprised to hear the words, not realizing she'd spoken out loud.

"What?" Philip questioned softly.

She shrugged, flustered for a moment. "You. Me. If you had come up to me yesterday and asked to buy me a drink, I probably would have refused."

He flashed a crooked grin. "I know. Why do you think I didn't?"

"Obviously you recognized that I was about to take the initiative," she said jokingly to hide her discomfort.

Together they turned and headed back toward the hotel, taking leisurely steps. Carla's bare toes kicked up the sand.

"What would you like to do tomorrow?" she asked, not because she was especially interested in their itinerary, but because knowing she would be seeing him in the morning would surely enhance her dreams tonight.

"Shall we get together for breakfast?"

"I'd like that."

Outside her door, Philip set a time and place for them to meet in the morning, then kissed her gently and left.

Carla walked slowly inside the room and released a long, drawn-out sigh. For such a rotten beginning, the day had turned out wonderfully well.

"Is that you, Carla?" The question came from the darkened interior of the room.

"No, it's the bogeyman," Carla teased.

"I take it you met someone?" Nancy's voice was soft and curious.

"Yup."

"Are you going to talk, or should I prepare to torture it out of you?" The moonlight silhouetted her roommate against the wall. Nancy was sitting on the side of the mattress.

"It's the guy I met yesterday." Carla couldn't disguise the wistful note in her voice.

"What happened? When I asked this morning, the looks you gave me said you didn't want to have anything to do with him."

"That was this morning."

Fluffing up her pillow, Nancy positioned it against the headboard, leaned against it and put her hands behind her head. "I'm glad things worked out."

"Me too." Carla moved into the room and began to undress."

"I can't believe how much I like Eduardo," Nancy said pensively as she stared dreamily at the ceiling. "I can't even begin to tell you what a marvelous day we had."

Carla slipped the silk nightie over her head. "The funny part was, I had no intention of seeing Philip again."

Nancy sighed unevenly and slid down so her head rested in the thick of the pillow. "He gave me a tour of Mazatlán that will hold memories to last a lifetime. And later tonight when he kissed me I could have cried, it was so incredibly beautiful.''

''But then Philip was there, and I'd been so miserable all day, and he suggested we have dinner, and not for the life of me could I refuse.''

''I've never felt this strongly about a man. And I've barely known Eduardo more than twenty-four hours.''

Carla pulled back the bedcovers and paused, holding the pillow to her stomach. ''I'm meeting Philip first thing in the morning.''

''Eduardo says he can't believe that someone as beautiful as I would be interested in him. And just because he broke his leg. He keeps assuring me he really isn't a klutz. As if I'd ever think such a thing.''

''I don't know if I'll be able to sleep. Every time I close my eyes I know Philip will be there. I don't know how to explain it. To look at him you'd be unimpressed. But he's the most gentle man. Tender.''

''I can't sleep. Every time I try, my heart hammers and I wonder if I'm going crazy to feel like this.''

The sheets felt cool against Carla's legs as she slipped between the covers and yawned. ''I guess I should get some sleep. Night, Nance.''

''Night,'' Nancy answered with a yawn of her own.

''By the way,'' Carla asked absently, ''how'd your day go?''

''Fantastic. How about you?''

''Wonderful.''

''I'm glad. Good night.''

''Night.''

Philip was already seated in the hotel restaurant when Carla arrived. Her gaze met his, and a smile played at the edges of her mouth as she enjoyed the way he was watching her. The sleeveless pink-and-blue crinkle-cotton sundress was her favorite, and she knew she looked good. She'd spent extra time with her makeup, and one glance from him confirmed that the effort had been well spent.

"Morning." Philip stood and pulled out her chair. "Did you sleep well?"

He leaned forward and kissed her cheek lightly. "Like a baby. How about you?"

Setting the large-brimmed straw hat on the empty seat beside her, Carla nodded. "Great."

The waiter appeared and handed them each a menu, but they didn't look at them. "What would you like to do today?"

"Explore," Carla replied immediately. "Would you mind if I dragged you to the arts and crafts center?"

Philip reached for her hand and squeezed it gently. "Not at all. And tomorrow I thought we'd take an excursion to Palmito de la Virgen."

Carla blinked. "Where?"

"An island near here. It's a bird-watcher's paradise."

The only bird Carla was interested in watching was Philip, but she didn't say as much.

"And Thursday I thought we might try our hand at deep-sea fishing."

"I'm game," she said, and giggled. "No pun intended."

"My, my, you're agreeable. Are you always like this in the mornings?"

Carla reached for the ice water, keeping her eyes lowered. "Most of the time."

"I'd like to discover that for myself."

The waiter arrived with his pen and pad, and Carla glanced up at him guiltily, realizing she hadn't even looked at the menu.

After breakfast they rode a pulmonia to the Mazatlán Arts and Crafts Center, and Philip insisted on buying her a lovely turquoise ring. Carla felt more comfortable purchasing her souvenirs from these people and not from the beach vendors. Here the price was set and there wasn't any haggling.

Tucking their purchases into a giant straw bag, Carla took off her hat and waved it in front of her face. Most of the shopping areas were air-conditioned, but once they stepped outside, the heat was stifling.

"Would you like something cool to drink?" Philip asked solicitously.

Smiling up at him, Carla placed a hand over her breast. "You, my dear man, know the path leading directly to my heart."

Unexpectedly, Philip's hand tightened on the back of her neck until his grip was almost painful. He dropped his hand and took a step forward as if he'd forgotten her completely. Surprised, but not alarmed, Carla reached for his arm. "What's wrong?"

"There's going to be a fight over there." He pointed to a group of youths who were having a heated exchange.

Although Carla couldn't understand what was being said, she assumed from the angry sound of their words that they would soon be coming to blows. Her gaze was drawn to Philip, and she was witness to an abrupt change in roles taking place within him. After all, she was a policeman's daughter. And Philip was an officer of the law. Once a cop, always a cop. He may be in Mazatlán, but he would never be entirely on vacation.

Philip's jaw hardened and his eyes narrowed with keen interest. Briefly he turned to her. "Stay here." The words were clipped and low and filled with an authority that would brook no resistance.

Carla wanted to argue. Everything inside urged her to scream that this was none of his business. What right did he have to involve himself with those youths? Mexico had its own police force. She watched as Philip strode briskly across the street toward the angry young men. He asked them something in Spanish, and even from this distance Carla could hear the authority in his voice. She hadn't a clue of what he was saying, but it didn't matter. It was the law-enforcement officer in him speaking, anyway, and she didn't want to know.

Only one thing prompted her to stay. If the situation got ugly and Philip needed help, she could scream or do something to get him out of this mess. But he didn't need her assistance, and a few minutes later the group broke up. With an amused grin, Philip jogged across the street to her side.

"That was—"

"I don't care to know, thank you," she announced frostily. Opening her large bag, she took out the several small items he'd purchased during their morning's outing.

"What's this?" He looked stunned.

"Your things," she answered without looking up. "You couldn't do it, could you?"

"Do what?"

Apparently he still didn't understand. "For once, just once, couldn't you have forgotten you're a cop? But no, Mr. Rescue had to speed to the scene of potential danger, defending truth and justice."

His face relaxed, and he reached for her. "Carla, couldn't you see—"

She sidestepped him easily. "You bet I saw," she shot back angrily. "You almost had me fooled, Philip Garrison. For a while there I actually believed we could have shared a wonderful vacation. But it's not going to work." Her voice was taut with building irritation. With unnecessary roughness, she dumped the packages into his arms. "Not even for a few days could either of us manage to forget what you are. Goodbye, Philip." She spun and ran across the street, waving her hand, hoping to attract a pulmonia driver. At least she could be grateful that Philip didn't make an effort to follow her. But that was little comfort . . . very little.

A pulmonia shot past her, and Carla stamped her foot childishly. She wished she had paid closer attention to the Spanish phrase Philip called to get the driver's attention.

Already she felt the perspiration breaking out across her face as she walked along the edge of the street. The late-morning sun could be torturous. Another driver approached, and Carla stepped off the curb and shouted something in Spanish, not sure what she'd said. With her luck, she mused wryly, it was probably something to do with Cookie Monster. But whatever it was worked because the driver immediately pulled to the curb.

"Hotel El Cid," she mumbled, hot and miserable.

"Sí, señorita, the man already say."

Man? Tossing a look over her shoulder, Carla found Philip standing on the other side of the street, studying her. He'd gotten the driver for her. If she hadn't been so blasted uncomfortable, she'd have told him exactly what he could do with his driver. As it was, all Carla wanted to do was escape. The sooner the better.

Her room was refreshingly cool when she returned. She threw herself across the bed and stared at the ceiling. Tears might have helped release some of her frustration, but she was too damn mad to cry.

After fifteen minutes, the hotel room gave her a bad case of claustrophobia. From her carryall Carla pulled the book she'd been reading on the airplane and opened the sliding glass door to the small balcony. A thorough inspection of the pool area revealed that Philip was nowhere in sight. Stuffing her book in her beach bag, Carla quickly changed into her swimsuit, slipping a cotton top over that and put on the straw hat. Not for anything was she going to allow Philip Garrison to ruin this vacation.

Carla was fortunate to find a vacant chaise longue. The pool was busy with the early-afternoon crowd. Several vacationers were in the water eating lunch at the counter that was built up against the pool's edge. Smiling briefly, Carla recalled her first glimpse of the submerged stools and wondered what this type of meal did to the theory of not swimming after eating.

Spreading out her towel, Carla raised the back of the lounger so that she could sit up comfortably and read. Her sunglasses had a tendency to slip down the bridge of her nose, and without much thought she pushed them back up. Philip's glasses did that occasionally. Angrily, she wiped his image from her mind and viciously turned the page of her suspense novel, nearly ripping it from the book.

An older man who was lying beside her stood, stretched and strolled lackadaisically toward the bar, apparently seeking something cool to drink. He was barely out of sight when a familiar voice spoke in her ear.

"Is this place taken?"

Carla's fingers gripped the page, but she didn't so much as acknowledge his presence. Without lifting her eyes from her book, she replied, "Yes, it is."

"That's fine, I'll just sit on the edge of the pool and chat," he replied casually.

Clenching her jaw so tight her teeth hurt, Carla turned a page, having no idea of what she had just read. "I'd appreciate it very much if you didn't."

Forcefully, Philip expelled his breath. "How long are you going to be unreasonable like this? All I'm asking is that you hear me out."

"How long?" Carla repeated mockingly. "You haven't got that much time. Never, as far as I'm concerned."

"Do you mean it?" The question was issued so low Carla had to strain to hear him.

Idly, she turned the next page. "Yes, I meant it," she replied.

"Okay." He took the towel, swung it around his neck and strolled away.

Carla felt a deep sense of disappointment settle over her. The least he could have done was argue with her! One would assume that after yesterday she meant more to him than that. But apparently not.

Without being obvious she glanced quickly around the pool area and discovered that Philip was nowhere in sight. Ten minutes later she did another survey. Nothing.

Tucking the book inside her beach bag, Carla settled back in her seat, joined her hands over her stomach and closed her eyes. A splash of water against her leg was more refreshing than irritating. But the cupful of water that landed on her upper thigh was a shock.

Gasping, she opened her eyes and sat up to brush the offending wetness away.

"Did I get water on you?" came the innocent question. "Please accept my apology."

"Philip Garrison, that was a rotten thing to do!" Inside she was singing. So he hadn't left.

"So was that last, untruthful remark."

"What remark?"

"That you never wanted to talk to me again." He lay down beside her on the chaise that had been previously taken by the older sunbather. "Obviously you did, or you wouldn't have made two deliberate inspections of the pool to see if I had left.''

Damn, she should have realized Philip had stayed and watched her. That was a rookie's trick. And clearly Philip was a seasoned officer. Rather than argue, she lifted her glasses and turned toward him with a smug look. ''I told you that place was taken,'' she said and repositioned herself so that the back of one hand rested against her brow. ''And I don't think he'd take kindly to you lying in his place when he returns.''

''Sure he would,'' Philip murmured confidently. ''Otherwise I wasted ten very good dollars.''

Struggling between outrage and delight, Carla sat up. ''Do you mean to say you bribed him?'' Her eyes widened as he nodded cheerfully. ''What do you think you're doing, Officer Garrison? First . . . first you spy on me and . . . then . . . and then . . .'' She sputtered. ''You bribe the man in the chair next to me. Just how low do you plan to stoop?''

Philip yawned. ''About that low.''

Carla did an admirable job of swallowing her laughter.

''I suspect you aren't as annoyed as you're letting on,'' Philip commented.

The humor died in her eyes. ''What makes you suggest that?''

''Well, you're still here, aren't you?''

Standing up, Carla pulled the thin cotton covering over her head. ''Not for long,'' she replied, and dived into the pool.

It felt marvelous. Swimming as far and for as long as she could under the aqua-blue water helped relieve some of her pent-up frustration. Finally she surfaced and sucked in a large breath of fresh air. In the glint of the sun, her hair was decidely red. Carla had hoped to avoid having Philip see it wet. Like everyone else, he was sure to comment on it. Swimming at night was preferable by far.

She'd barely caught her breath when Philip surfaced beside her. Treading water at his side, she offered him a tremulous smile. "I really was angry this morning. I behaved childishly to run off like that. Thank you for seeing that I got a ride back to the hotel."

Their eyes met, and he smiled lovingly at her. "I know how angry you were; that's why I didn't follow you. But given time, I figured you'd forgive me." His arms found her waist and brought her close to him. Their feet kicked in unison, keeping them afloat.

"I'll forgive you on one condition," she stated firmly, and looped her arms around his neck. "You've got to promise not to do that again. Please, Philip. For me, leave your police badge in your room. We're in Mexico, and they have their own defenders of justice."

Philip went still, and she could feel him become tense. The sparkle faded from his eyes as they darkened and became more intense. "Carla, I'll do my best, but I can't change what I am."

Her grip around his neck relaxed, and with a sense of defeat she lowered her eyes. "But don't you see? I can't, either," she murmured miserably, and her voice fell to a whisper.

His hold tightened as he brought his body intimately close to hers in the water. "But we can try."

"What would be the use?"

"Oh, I don't know," he said softly, and brushed aside the offending strands of wet hair from her cheek. "I can think of several things." His lips replaced his fingers, and he blazed a trail of infinitely sweet kisses along her brow and eyes, working his way to her mouth.

For an instant, Carla was caught in the rapture of his touch, but an abrupt noise behind them brought her to her senses. Breaking free, she shook her head. "I . . . I don't know, Philip. I want to think on it."

"Okay, that sounds fair."

He didn't have to be so agreeable! At least he could have argued with her. With a little sigh, Carla turned away and said, "I think I'll go to my room and lie down for a while. The sun does me in fairly easily." She started to swim away, then rapidly changed direction and joined Philip. "I almost forgot something," she murmured as she covered his mouth with hers and kissed him thoroughly.

Obviously shaken, Philip blinked twice. "What was that for?" he asked, and cleared his throat.

"For not mentioning my hair color."

He cocked his head, and a puzzled frown marred his brow. "There are several other things I haven't mentioned that you may wish to thank me for."

"Later," she said with a small laugh.

"Definitely later."

Chapter Four

Amazingly, Carla did sleep most of the afternoon. She hadn't realized how exhausted she was. The sun, having taken its toll, had faded by the time she stirred. A glance at the clock told Carla that it was dinnertime. Although she hadn't made any arrangements to meet Philip, she knew he'd be looking for her.

Dressing quickly, she hunted for her sandals, crawling on the floor. Finally she located them under the bed and was on her way into the bathroom to see what she could do with her hair when something stopped her. The faint sound of someone singing in Spanish drifted in past the balcony door that had been left ajar. Those deep male tones were unmistakable.

After eagerly parting the drapes, Carla opened the sliding glass door farther. The music and voice grew stronger, and the lovingly familiar voice sang loudly off key.

"Philip!"

Standing below, playing a guitar and singing at the top of his voice was crazy, wonderful Philip. A band of curious onlookers had gathered around him. Now, however, they focused their attention on her.

"You idiot," she cried. "What are you doing?"

"Serenading you," he shouted back, completely serious. "Do you like it?"

"I'd like it a lot better if you sang on key."

He strummed a few bars. "Can't have everything. Are you hungry?"

"Starved. I'd eat turtle tacos."

"You must be famished. Hurry down, will you? I think someone might arrest me."

Stuffing her hair under her straw hat, Carla bounded down the stairs. She paused on the bottom step, straightened her dress and took a deep breath. Then, feeling more composed, she turned the corner and found Philip relaxing on a chaise longue.

"Hi," she said, fighting the breathlessness that weakened her voice.

He rose to his feet with an ease many would envy. "I must have sounded better than I thought."

"What makes you think that?"

A grin played at the edges of his mouth as he dug inside his pocket and pulled out a handful of loose change. "People were obviously impressed. Soon after you went back inside, several started throwing coins my way."

Fighting back the bubbling laughter, Carla looped her arm around his elbow. "I hate to disappoint you,

Philip, but I have the distinct feeling they were paying you *not* to sing."

The sound of his laughter tugged at her heart. "Where are we going for dinner? I wasn't teasing about being hungry."

"Anyplace you say." Tucking her hand more securely in the crook of his arm, he escorted her through the hotel to the series of stairs that led to the busy street below.

"Anyplace I say," she repeated. "My, my, you're agreeable all of a sudden."

"With a beautiful girl on my arm, and my pockets full of change, why shouldn't I be?"

"No reason."

"Then dinner wherever the lady chooses."

"Well, I suppose I'd better choose a restaurant where I won't have to take off my hat. I didn't wash my hair after our dip in the pool this afternoon, and now it resembles Raggedy Ann's."

"Then it's perfect for what I have in mind," he said with an enigmatic toss of his head. Sandy locks of hair fell across his brow and he brushed them aside.

"Well, are you going to tell me, or do I have to guess?" she asked with a hint of impatience. She noticed that Philip had a way of arousing her curiosity, then dropping the subject. Her father did the same thing, and Carla briefly wondered if this was a common trait among policemen. They didn't want to give out too much information—keep the world guessing, seemed to be their intent. Other things about Philip reminded her of her father. He was a kind, concerned man. Like her father, he cared when the rest of the world didn't want to be bothered.

"Ever hear of La Gruta de Cerro del Creston?" Philip asked, snapping her out of deep thought.

"He was some general, right?"

"Wrong," he responded with a trace of droll tolerance. "It's a cave where, it's rumored, pirates used to store their treasure. Stolen treasure, of course. It's only accessible at low tide, but I thought we might pick up a picnic lunch and eat along the beach. Later, when the tide is low, we can explore the cave."

Carla's interest was piqued. "That sounds great."

"And of course there's always the advantage of having you to myself in a deep, dark cave."

"Honestly, Garrison, cool your hormones," she said jokingly.

One of the hot-rod golf carts Philip enjoyed so much delivered them close to the lighthouse near the heart of the city. Holding her hat, Carla climbed out from the back of the cart. Her senses were spinning, and she doubted if she'd ever get used to riding in those suicidal contraptions. The short rides weren't so bad, but anything over three miles was like a death wish.

A drop of rain hit her hand. Carla raised her eyes to examine the darkening sky and groaned inwardly. A storm would ruin everything. Besides, if Philip saw what happened to her hair in the rain, she'd never live it down. The frizzies invariably gave her a striking resemblance to the bride of Frankenstein.

"Philip?"

Preoccupied for the moment, Philip paid the driver and returned the folded money to his pocket. "Something wrong?"

"It's raining."

"I know."

Twisting the strap of her purse, she swung it over her shoulder and secured the large-brimmed straw hat by holding it down over both ears. "Maybe we should go back to the hotel."

"Why?"

She swallowed nervously. "Well, we obviously can't have a picnic in the rain, and if...my hat should come off...well, my hair—"

Suddenly, the sky opened up and the earth was bombarded with heavy sheets of rain. Giving a cry of alarm, Carla ran for shelter. Mud splashed against the back of her legs, and immediately a chill ran up her arms.

Philip caught up with her and cupped her elbow. "Let's get out of here."

"Where?" she shouted, but he didn't answer as they raced down a side street. After two long blocks, Carla stopped counting. Placing one foot in front of the other was all that she could manage in the torrent that was beating against her.

Philip led her into a building and up two flights of stairs.

Leaning against the hallway wall, Carla gasped for breath. "Where are we?"

"My parents' condo."

Vaguely, she recalled Philip mentioning that the condo was the reason he was in Mazatlán. He'd said something about repairs, but Carla didn't care where they were as long as it was dry.

"Let's get these wet things off," Philip suggested, holding the door open for her and leading the way into the kitchen.

The condominium looked surprisingly modern, and Carla hurried inside, not wishing to leave a trail of mud across the cream-colored carpet. The washer and dryer were behind a louvered door. Philip pulled his shirt from his waist and unbuttoned it. "We'd better let these dry."

Wide-eyed, her mouth open, Carla watched him toss his drenched shirt inside. He paused and glanced expectantly at her.

"You don't honestly expect me to parade around here in my underwear, do you?"

"Well, to be honest," he said with a wry grin, "I didn't expect it, but I was hoping. Hold on and I'll get you my mom's robe."

By the time he returned, Carla had removed her sandals and found a kitchen towel to dry her feet. When she heard Philip approach, she straightened and continued to press her hat—still secure despite everything—down over her ears.

"Here." He draped the cotton robe over a chair. "I'll start a fire. Let me know when you're finished."

Shivering, Carla slipped the dress over her hips and tossed it inside the dryer. Another towel served as a turban for her hair and hid the effects of the rain.

She tied the sash of the robe and took a deep breath. Self-consciously, she stood just outside the living room. A small fire was crackling in the fireplace, and

Philip was kneeling in front of it adding one stick of wood at a time.

He seemed to sense that she was watching him. "How do you feel?" He stood and crossed the room, joining her. Placing a hand on each shoulder, he smiled into her eyes. "Mother's robe never looked so good."

"I feel like a drowned rat." The turban slipped over one eye, and Carla righted it quickly.

His hands found the side of her neck, and his touch sent a warm sensation through her. "Believe me when I say you don't look like one."

They continued to regard each other, and Carla's heart began to pound like a locomotive racing against time. In some ways she and Philip were doing that. There were only a few days left of their vacation, and then it would be over. It had to be.

"Come in and sit down," Philip said at last, and his thumb traced her lips in a feather-light caress. "The fire should take the chill from your bones."

"I'm . . . not really cold." Not when you're touching me, she added silently.

"Me neither."

Carla was convinced his thoughts were an echo of her own.

"Hungry?"

"Not really." Not anymore.

"Good."

Together they sat on the plush love seat that was angled to face the fireplace. Philip's arm reached for her, bringing her within the haven of his embrace.

Resting her head against the curve of his shoulder, Carla let her fingers toy with the dark hairs on his bare chest. Her body was in contact with his chest, hips and thighs, and whenever they touched, she could feel a heat building. She struggled to control her breathing so Philip wouldn't guess the effect he was having on her.

"I poured these while you were changing," Philip murmured, his voice low and slightly husky. He leaned forward and reached for the two glasses of wine sitting on the polished oak coffee table.

Straightening, Carla accepted the long-stemmed crystal glass with a smile of appreciation and tasted the wine. It was an excellent sweet variety with a fragrant bouquet.

Removing the glass from her unresisting fingers, Philip set it aside. As he leaned back, his jaw brushed her chin, and his warm breath caressed her face. The contact stopped them both. He hadn't meant it to be sensual, Carla was sure of that, but her heart thumped wildly. Closing her eyes, she inhaled a quivering breath.

"Philip?" she whispered.

His mouth explored the side of her neck, sending rapturous shivers up and down her spine. "Yes?"

"Did you arrange for the rainstorm?" Carla couldn't believe how low and sultry her voice sounded.

"No, but I'm glad it happened."

Carla was, too, but she wouldn't admit it. She didn't need to.

Gently, Philip pressed her backward so that her head rested against the arm of the sofa; then his mouth claimed the wine sweetness of her lips. His kiss was slow, leisurely and far more intoxicating than mere wine.

Drawing in a shaky breath, Philip diverted his attention to her neck, nuzzling the scented hollow of her throat. His hands wandered over her hips, artfully arousing her so that she shifted, seeking more. She wanted to give more of herself and take more at the same time. Her restless hands explored his back, reveling in the tightness of his corded muscles. This man was deceptively strong. Her fingers found a scar, and she longed to kiss it.

Gradually, the heat that had begun to flow through her at the tenderness of his touch spread to every part of her; her flesh felt feverishly warm. But when Philip's hands slid across her abdomen, she tensed slightly. He murmured her name, and his mouth lingered on her lips, moving from one side of her mouth to the other in a deep, sensuous exploration that left her weak and clinging. Without rushing, his hands glided upward to the soft undersides of her breasts. When he teased her nipples with his fingers, Carla nearly cried out in sheer rapture.

Philip turned her so that she was sitting half-upright. As he did so, the towel that was covering her hair twisted and fell forward across her face. Gently, Philip lifted the offending material off her face, but her desperate hold on it prevented him from tossing it aside.

"Can we get rid of this thing?" he asked gently.

"No." She struggled to sit completely up. Both hands secured the terry-cloth towel.

"Your hair can't be that bad," he coaxed.

"It's worse. Turn around," she demanded as she leaned forward and rewound the turban. "I... I don't want you to see it."

Expelling his breath, Philip leaned against the back of the sofa and closed his eyes. "Would you feel better if you showered and dried those precious locks?"

She nodded eagerly.

"Come on, I'm sure Mom's got something in the bathroom that should help."

Carla followed him down a long, narrow hallway that led to a bathroom. Investigating the vanity drawers, he managed to come up with a blow-dryer and curling iron.

"I think my sister gave this to her for Christmas last year."

Carla's heart sank. "But I can't use this. The package isn't even open."

With a crooked grin, Philip tore off the cellophane. "If it bothers you, I'll tell her I used it."

Carla giggled delightedly. "I'd like to hear her answer to that."

Removing several fluffy towels from the hall closet, Philip handed them to her. "While you're making yourself beautiful I'm going to make us something to eat."

Hugging the fresh towels, Carla gave him a grateful smile. "Thank you, Philip. I honestly mean that."

He shrugged and pushed his glasses up the bridge of his nose. "Are you sure you don't need someone to wash your back?" he asked in a low, seductive voice.

"I'm sure." But the look he gave her as he turned toward the kitchen was enough to inflame her senses. Never had she felt this strongly about anyone after such a short time. Maybe that was normal. They had only a week together, and already three of those precious days had been spent. All too soon the time would come when she'd say goodbye to him at the airport. And it would be goodbye.

The water felt fantastic as it sprayed against her soft skin. When she'd finished showering, she put the robe on and opened the bathroom door to allow the steam to escape.

"Your dress is dry if you want me to bring it to you," Philip called to her from the kitchen.

"Give me a minute," she shouted back. Carla's russet-red curls were blown dry and tamed with the curling iron in record time. Her face was void of makeup, and she knew she looked much paler than usual, but one kiss from Philip would correct that.

Tying the sash of the robe as she walked across the living-room carpet, Carla sniffed the delicate aroma drifting from the kitchen.

"Mushrooms," she announced, and picked one out of the sizzling butter with her long fingernails and popped it into her mouth.

"Canned, I'm afraid."

"No problem, I like mushrooms any way they come." She lifted out another and fed it to Philip. His shirt was dry and tucked neatly into his waistband. Her dress, she'd noticed, was hanging off a knob from the kitchen cabinet.

Peeking inside the oven, she turned around delightedly. "I don't suppose those are T-bone steaks under
the grill?"

"Yup, but they'll take time. I had to get them out of
the freezer." Philip set the cooking fork beside the
skillet and reached for her. His large hands almost
spanned her waist. "But then we have lots of time."

But not nearly enough, her heart answered.

Hours later, after they'd consumed an entire bottle
of wine and eaten their fill, they washed and dried the
dishes. Soft music played romantically in the background.

"Philip?" Carla tilted her head as she released the
plug from the sink to drain the soapy water.

He looked at her expectantly. "Hmm?"

"There's a scar on your back. I don't think I'd noticed it before. What happened?" she asked curiously.

"It's nothing." He stooped down to place the skillet in the bottom cupboard.

"It didn't feel like it. It's long and narrow,
like . . . like . . ." She stopped cold. A painful sensation in the pit of her stomach viciously attacked her,
and she leaned weakly against the counter. "Like a
knife. You were stabbed, weren't you?"

Lifting up the frames of his glasses, Philip pinched
the bridge of his nose. "Damn," he uttered savagely.

"You didn't want me to know. Well, I do now," she
cried, and gestured defiantly with her hand. "What
happened? Did you decide to step in and break up a
gang war all by yourself? You were willing to try your

hand at that this morning." Her voice shook uncontrollably with fearful anger.

"No, it wasn't anything like that. I was—"

"I don't want to hear. Don't tell me." She searched frantically for her hat, storming across one room and into the other.

"First you demand to know, then you shout you don't. I hope you realize how unreasonable you sound," he said with a low growl.

"I...don't care what I sound like." Her hat was beside her purse in the other room, and she practically raced to it. "One look at you and I should have known you were bad news. But oh, no, I had to follow this crazy scheme of Nancy's and make a complete idiot of myself. It's not going to work, Philip. Not for another day. Not for a week. Not at all. I'm going back to the hotel."

"Carla, will you listen to me?" Philip stuffed his hands into his pants pockets, and his face hardened with a grimness she hadn't expected to see in him. "It's working, believe me, it's working."

"Maybe everything is fine for you. But I don't want to get involved. Not with you."

"You're already involved."

Defiantly, she crossed her arms in front of her. "Not anymore." Mentally and emotionally, she would have to block him out of her life before the pain became too great.

"That's twice in one day."

"Don't you see?" she cried as if shouting helped prove her point. "All right, all right, I conceded the point. I could like you very much. It probably wouldn't take very much to fall in love with you, but I just can't. Look at me, Philip." Tossing her head back, she held out her hands, palms down, for his inspection. "I'm shaking because already I care enough for you to worry about a stabbing that happened before we even met."

"Being knifed is the only thing that's ever happened to me. I was a rookie, and stupid...."

"This is supposed to reassure me?" she retorted, jamming her hat on top of her head.

He followed her to the front door and pressed a shoulder against the wood to prevent her from opening it. "Carla, for heaven's sake, will you listen to reason?"

Hands clenched at her side, she emitted a frustrated sigh. Tears blurred her vision, and pain clawed at her chest. She didn't expect him to understand. "It was hopeless from the beginning."

"I'm not letting you leave until you listen to me."

Carla breathed out, her lungs aching from the effort to control her emotion. "Philip, I like you so much." Of its own volition, her hand found and explored the side of his jaw. She could feel his muscles tense as her fingertips investigated the rough feel of his day-old beard. "I won't forget you," she whispered shakily.

His hand captured hers and moved it to his mouth so that he could kiss the tender skin of her palm. As if he'd burned her, Carla jerked her fingers free.

"Come on, I'll take you back to the hotel." His quiet determination penetrated her resolve. She knew him well enough to realize arguing would do her little good.

Philip didn't say a word on the entire trip back. They passed a horse-drawn carriage, and Carla wanted to weep at the sight of the two young lovers who sat in the back with their arms entwined. What a perfect end to a lovely day such a ride would have been. Philip gave her a look that said he was reading her thoughts. They could have been that couple.

Bowing her head, Carla studied her clenched hands, all too aware that Philip thought she was overreacting. But she couldn't ask him to be something he wasn't, and she couldn't change, either.

His hand cupped her elbow as she climbed the short series of stairs that led to the hotel lobby. Halfway through the lobby, Carla paused and murmured, "I'll say goodbye here."

"No, you won't. I'll escort you to your room."

When they reached her door, Carla's fingers nervously fumbled with the purse latch. Her hand closed around the key, and she drew in a deep, shuddering breath.

"I know you're angry," she said without looking up. Her gaze was centered on the room key. "And to be honest, I don't blame you. Thank you for today and yesterday. I'll never think of Mexico without remembering you." The brittle smile she gave him as she glanced up took more of an effort than he would ever know.

The edges of Philip's mouth were drawn faintly upward, and Carla guessed that he wasn't in any more of a mood to smile than she was.

Her hand twisted the doorknob.

"What? No farewell kiss. Surely I deserve that much."

Carla meant only to brush her lips over his. Not to tease, but to disguise the very real physical attraction she felt for him. But as she raised her mouth, his hand cupped the back of her head and she was crushed in his embrace. Where Philip had always been gentle, now he was urgent, greedily devouring her lips with a hunger that left her so weak she clung to him. She wanted to twist away but realized that if she struggled, Philip would release her. Instead, her arms crept around his neck, and timidly her tongue played with his. Philip groaned aloud and gathered her as close as physical boundaries would allow, his arms crushing her.

A trembling weakness attacked her, and Philip altered his method of assault. His tongue passed slowly along her parted lips, and he kissed her leisurely, with a thoroughness that made her ache for more. He didn't rush but seemed to savor each second, content to have her break the contact.

She did, but only when she thought her lungs would burst.

"Goodnight, Carla," he whispered against her ear, and opened the door for her.

Carla would have stumbled inside if Philip hadn't caught her. With as much dignity as possible, she tore herself free, entered the room unaided and closed the door on Philip without looking back.

The cool, dark interior contained no welcome. The taste of Philip's kiss was on her mouth, and the male scent of him lingered, disturbing her further.

Pacing the floor did little to relieve the ache. Desperately, she tried watching television and was irrationally angry that every station had programs in Spanish.

After her long afternoon nap she wasn't tired. Nor was she interested in visiting the party scene that was taking place in the lounge and bars.

Her frustration mounted with every second. Standing on the balcony that overlooked the pool area, she noted again that there wasn't anyone around. A gentle breeze stirred the evening air and contained a freshness that often follows a storm. The first night she'd arrived and met Philip they had swum. And the pool had been fantastic.

Laps would help, and with the heavy tourist crowds that filled the pool during the day, it would be impossible to do them in the morning. Besides, if she tired herself out, she might be able to sleep.

Determined now, she located a fresh suit in the bottom of her carryall and hurriedly undressed. Tomorrow would be filled with avoiding Philip, but she didn't want to think about that now.

The water was refreshingly cool as she dived in and broke the surface twenty feet later. Her arms carried her to the far side, and the first lap was accomplished with a drive born of angry remorse. There wasn't anyone to blame for this but herself. She'd known almost from the beginning what Philip was. He hadn't tried to disguise it.

Her shoulders heaving as she struggled for breath ten long laps later, Carla stood in the shallow end and brushed the hair from her face.

"I didn't think you'd be able to stay away," Philip said, standing beside her. "I couldn't either."

Chapter Five

Carla froze, her hands in her hair. Philip was right. When she'd come to the pool, the thought had played in the back of her mind that he would be there, too. For all her self-proclaimed righteousness, she didn't want their time together to end with an argument.

The worst part was that she'd overreacted, and like an immature child, she'd run away. "I'm sorry about tonight," she murmured in a voice that was quiveringly soft. "But when I realized how you'd gotten that scar, I panicked."

Philip turned her around so that they faced each other standing waist deep in the pool's aqua-blue water. "You don't need to explain. I know."

The moon's gentle radiance revealed a thin film of moisture glistening on his torso. Carla longed to touch him. "Turn around," she requested softly, and when he did, she slid her arms around his waist, just below the water line, and pressed her cheek against the curve of his spine. Almost shyly, her fingers located the scar, and she bent down and kissed it gently. The next time, Philip might not be so fortunate; such a blade could end his life. The thought was sobering, and a chill raced up Carla's arms.

"We agreed to a week," Philip reminded her as he twisted around and looped his arms over her shoulder. "This vacation is for us. Our lives, our jobs, our friends are back in Washington. But we're here. Nothing's going to spoil what we have for the remainder of the week." He said it with a determination she couldn't deny.

Nothing will ruin it, Carla's heart responded. Everything was already ruined, her head shouted.

They swam for an hour, making excuses to touch each other, kissing when the time seemed right. And it often seemed right.

The night had been well spent when they made arrangements to meet again in the morning. Silently, Carla climbed into the bed across from her sleeping friend. A glance at her watch told her it was after two. This time she had no trouble falling into a restful slumber.

The early-morning sounds of Nancy brushing her teeth and dressing woke Carla when the sun was barely up. Struggling to a sitting position, Carla raised her arms high above her head and yawned. "What time is it?"

"Six," Nancy whispered. "Eduardo and I are flying to Puerto Vallarta. I probably won't be back until late tonight."

Carla nodded and settled back into her bed, hugging the thick pillow.

"And before I forget, I have an invitation for you and ... your friend."

"Philip," Carla supplied.

"Right." Nancy laughed lightly. "Who says my head isn't in the clouds? Anyway, you're both invited to dinner with Eduardo and me Saturday evening."

Carla's eyes remained closed, and she nuzzled the covers over her shoulder. "Sounds nice, I'll mention it to Philip." Her lashes fluttered open. "That's our last day here."

"It's really going by quickly, isn't it?" The sad note in Nancy's voice couldn't be disguised. "We've got only three more days."

"Three days," Carla repeated sleepily.

"But you have to admit, this has been our best vacation."

And our worst, Carla mused. Every year she hoped to have a holiday fling. But not next year. Her heart couldn't take this. Of course, not everyone would affect her the way Philip had, but she wasn't game to have her hopes dashed every year.

"By the way, did you hear the gossip that was going around the hotel yesterday?" Nancy didn't wait for Carla's answer. "Some crazy American was standing by the pool serenading a girl with love songs. Apparently, she's staying at the hotel."

For the third time that morning, Carla's eyes opened. A faint color began an ascent up her neck to her cheeks. "Some crazy American?"

"Right, an American. Isn't that the most incredibly romantic thing you've ever heard? Women would kill for a man like that."

"I think you're right." Carla's interest was aroused as she sat up. "Allow me to introduce you to some crazy American Saturday night."

"Philip?"

"You got it." Carla blinked twice. "And it was romantic, except that everyone at the pool was staring at us."

Nancy sighed and sat on the end of Carla's mattress. "Eduardo's romantic like that." She smoothed a wrinkle from her white cotton pants as she crossed her legs. "He says the most beautiful things to me. But half the time I don't know whether to believe him or not. The lines sound so practised, and yet he appears sincere."

"In instances like that only time will tell," Carla said without thinking.

"But that's something we don't have. In three days I'll be flying home, and I bet I never hear from Eduardo again."

Carla searched her friend's coolly composed face, interpreting the doubts. "But I thought we were only looking for a little romance to liven up our holiday."

Nancy sighed expressively, and her eyes grew wary. "I was, but you know what? I think there's something basically wrong with me. For years now, you and I have had this dream of the perfect vacation. We've been to Southern California, Reno, Hawaii and now Mazatlán. Every year we plan one week when we can let down our hair and have a good time." She paused, and her shoulders sagged in a gesture of defeat. "We do it so that when we get back to Seattle and our neat, orderly lives, we'll have something to get us through another dull year."

"But it's never worked out that way. Our vacations are as dull as our lives."

"I know," Nancy agreed morosely. "Until this year, and all of sudden I discover I'm not the type for a one-week fling. I'll never be the 'love 'em and leave 'em' type. I like Eduardo, and as far as I can tell, he likes me. But I could be one of any number of women he escorts during the course of a summer. He sees a fun-seeking American on vacation, and I doubt that he'd recognize the hardworking high school teacher that I really am." Nancy sighed and ran her fingers through her hair in frustration. "The funny part is that after all these years this was exactly what I thought I wanted. And now that I've met Eduardo I can see how wrong I've been. When I meet a man I want a meaningful relationship that will grow. Not a one-week fling."

Carla wasn't surprised by her friend's insights. Nancy often saw things more clearly than she did, whereas she, Carla, often reacted more to her emotions. Remembering last night and the way she'd panicked at the knowledge that Philip had been stabbed produced a renewed sense of regret. With Philip her emotions had done a lot of reacting lately.

Later, when they met for an excursion to the Palmito de la Virgen, the bird-watchers' island in the bay, Carla mentioned Eduardo's invitation to dinner. Philip was agreeable, as she knew he would be.

The following morning, Philip and Carla went deep-sea fishing at the crack of dawn. Philip managed to bring in a large tuna, but all Carla caught was a bad case of seasickness.

"It wasn't the boat rocking so much," she explained later, "but the way the captain killed that poor fish, cut him up and passed him around for everyone to sample—*raw*."

"It's a delicacy."

"Not to me."

On their last afternoon together, while Carla stood terrified on the beach, Philip went para-sailing. With her eyes tightly shut, his glasses clenched in her hand, she waited until he was in the air before she chanced a look. Even then her heart hammered in her throat, and she struggled to beat down the fear that threatened to overcome her. Philip had to be crazy to allow his life to hang by a thin line. The only thing keeping him airborne was a motor boat and a cord that was attached from the boat to the parachute.

Her fear was transmitted as an irrational form of anger. The worst part was that Carla realized she was reacting to her emotions again. She wanted Philip to behave like a normal, safe and sane male. Who would have believed that a lanky guy who wore horn-rimmed glasses defied death every day of his life?

Carla was exactly where Philip had left her when he returned. The stem of his glasses had made deep indentations in her fingers, and she didn't need to be told she was deathly pale.

Exhilarated, Philip ran to her side and took his glasses from her hand. "It was fantastic," he said, wiping the sea water from his face with a towel and placing it in her beach bag.

She gave him a poor imitation of a smile and lied. "It looked like fun."

"Then why do you resemble a Halloween ghost?"

"It frightened me," she admitted, and was grateful he didn't mention that she looked as if she were going to burst into tears.

"Carla, I was watching you from up there. You were more than frightened. You looked like a statue with your eyes closed and your teeth clenched, standing there frightened out of your wits."

"I thought you couldn't see without your glasses," she responded, only slightly piqued.

"My vision is affected only close up. I saw how terrified you were."

"I told you before, I'm a conservative person." She didn't enjoy being on the defensive.

"You're more conservative than a pin-striped suit," he growled. "There's nothing reckless in para-sailing."

"And that's your opinion." Impatiently, she picked up her beach towel, stuffed it in her bag and turned away.

"The most daring thing you've done since we arrived is eat chicken in chocolate sauce," Philip insisted, rushing up beside her.

If he wanted to fight, she wasn't going to back down. "What do you want from me, anyway?" she cried.

He slapped his hands against his sides. "I don't know. I guess I'd like for you to recognize that there's

more to life than self-actualization through checkers.''

Her hand flew to her hip, and she glared at him with
a fierceness that stole her breath. "You know, I really
tried to be the good sport. Everything you've wanted
to do, including risking my life in that...that ocean
surf." She waved her finger at the incoming tide.
"Deep-sea fishing...everything. How can you say
those things to me?''

"For heaven's sake, people come from all over the
world to swim in this ocean. What makes it so dangerous for you?''

Several moments passed before she'd gained enough
control of her voice to speak. "The very first day we
arrived you warned me that the current was too strong
for swimming.''

"It was." He pointed to a green flag beside the life-
guard station. "The flag was red.''

"Oh." Carla swallowed and forged ahead, weaving
her way around the sunbathing beauties that dotted
the beach. "Why didn't you explain that at the time?''
she demanded.

Curious stares followed her as she ran up the concrete steps that led to the hotel's outdoor restaurant.
Not waiting for Philip, she pulled out a chair and sat
down, purposely placing her beach bag in the empty
chair beside her.

Philip joined her, taking his short-sleeve shirt out of
her bag and impatiently stuffing his arms into the
sleeve.

"And I suppose you're going to make a big deal out of the fact I didn't want to eat raw fish or dance on my hat," Carla cried, incensed. "I'll have you know—"

Before she could finish, the waiter came for their order. To prove a point, Carla defiantly asked for the hotel special, a hollowed-out coconut filled with a frothy alcoholic concoction. Philip looked at her in surprise, then ordered a cup of coffee.

"Carla," he said after the waiter had left, "what the hell are you doing? You'll be under the table before you finish that drink. There must be sixteen ounces of booze in that coconut."

Gritting her teeth, Carla slowly shook her head. "Everything I do is wrong. There's no satisfying you, is there? If you find me so dull and boring, why have you insisted we spend this week together?"

"I don't find you dull." The paper straw he was fingering snapped in two.

"Then...then why are you so angry with me? What have I done?"

Philip ran a hand across his eyes. "Because, dammit, I know what's coming. We're leaving in the morning, and when we arrive in Seattle it's goodbye, Philip. With no regrets and no looking back."

"But we agreed—"

"I know what we agreed," he growled. "But I didn't count on... Dammit, I didn't mean for any of this to come out this way. I think I'm falling in love with you."

Carla felt the air rush out of her. "Oh, Philip, you can't make a statement like that after only knowing me a week."

"Six days," he corrected grimly, and stared at her. His anger was barely in check, even now, when he'd admitted his feelings. "I'm not all that versed in love," he said stiffly. "Nicole was evidence of that. And if the truth be known, I thought for a long time afterward that there'd never be another woman I'd care about as much. But what I feel for you grows stronger every minute we're together. We have something special, Carla, and your cautious, conservative fears are going to ruin it."

The waiter delivering their drinks silenced Philip. Carla stared at hers. Normally she didn't drink during the day, but Philip's accusations had hurt. She took a tentative sip from the alcohol-filled coconut and winced. Philip was right; she was a fool to have ordered it.

"I can see what's going to happen," he continued. "And I don't like it."

Confusion raced through her. Philip was saying the very things she'd dreaded most—and most longed to hear. "Don't you attribute this attraction to the lure of the forbidden?" She sought a sane argument. "You knew from the beginning how I feel about cops and law enforcement...and maybe in the back of your mind you thought I would change."

"No," he answered starkly. "Maybe the thought flitted through my mind at one time. But I felt that chemistry between us before you ever told me about your father."

"That soon? Philip, we'd only just met."

Her answer didn't appear to please him. "Don't you think I've told myself that a thousand times?"

The silence stretched between them, tight and unbearable. Carla shifted in her seat and pushed her drink aside. Tonight was their last night, and they were going to spend it fighting. She was more than half in love with him herself, but she couldn't let Philip know that, especially since she had no intention of continuing to see him after they returned. What was the use? He wouldn't change, and she couldn't. There was no sense in dragging out the inevitable.

"I think I'll go up and get ready for tonight," she said, struggling to keep her voice level.

Philip didn't try to stop her as she stood, reached for her beach bag and walked away. Tears had filled her eyes by the time she reached her room. Pressing her index finger under her eye helped stop the brimming emotion. Somehow, with a smile on her face, she'd make it through tonight and tomorrow. When the time came, she'd thank Philip for a marvelous week and kiss him goodbye. And mean it.

A careful application of her cosmetics helped disguise the fact that she'd spent a good portion of the afternoon fighting back tears. Carla thought she'd done a good job until Nancy came into the room to change, took one look at her friend and declared:

"You've been crying."

"Oh, damn!" Carla raced to the bathroom mirror. "How'd you know?"

"It was either the puffy red eyes or the extra makeup. Honestly, Carla, with a complexion like yours you can't help but tell."

"Great. Now what am I going to do?"

Nancy inspected her closet, finally deciding on a pale-blue sleeveless dress with spaghetti straps. "The same thing I'll probably end up doing. Smile and say how much you're going to miss Mexico and how this has been the best vacation of your life." She turned and laid the dress across the bed. "Now that's what you're supposed to tell everyone else. What you say to me is the truth."

"Philip claims he's falling in love with me," she declared, and sniffled loudly. Fresh tears formed, and she grabbed a tissue and forced her head back to stare at the ceiling, hoping to discourage any new tear tracks from ruining her makeup.

"And that makes you cry. I thought you really liked Philip."

"But there's something I didn't tell you. Philip's a cop." She didn't need to say another word.

"Good grief, Carla, how do you get yourself into these things?"

"I don't know," she lamented, pressing the tissue under her eyes. "Philip was so open and honest about it when he didn't have to be, and when he suggested that we enjoy this week I couldn't turn him down. He's wonderful. Everything about him is wonderful."

"Except that he's a cop."

"And he's amazingly like my dad. It doesn't matter where either one of them is, the badge is always on. Even when we were shopping, Philip stopped and broke up a potential fight. Worse, Philip's been stabbed once because he was careless."

"Your dad was hurt not long ago, wasn't he?" Nancy asked from her position on the end of the bed.

"Once. He was chasing a suspect, fell and broke his arm."

Nancy nodded. "I remember because you were so furious with him."

"And with good reason. Dad's too old to be out there running after men twenty years younger than he."

"Take my advice and don't tell him that." Nancy's comment was punctuated with a soft laugh.

Carla decided that Nancy knew her father better than most people did. "Don't worry, Mom said it for me."

An abrupt knock on the door caused them both to glance curiously at one another. Carla's watch told her it was forty-five minutes before they were scheduled to meet the men.

Since she was ready, Carla answered the door. "Philip!" she exclaimed in surprise. How good he looked in a suit and tie! And his eyes were the deepest gray she could remember seeing. One glance at her, and their color intensified even more.

"I thought you might be ready," he said stiffly.

"Yes... I am."

"Would you have a drink with me in the lounge? Nancy and Eduardo can join us there."

He sounded as if he were preparing to read Carla her rights. "Sure," she replied, and tossed a look over her shoulder to Nancy. "We'll meet you in the lounge."

Nancy arched both brows expressively. "See you there."

Philip didn't say a word until after they'd ordered their drinks. "I owe you an apology."

Carla's smile wavered only slightly as she reached for his hand. "You can't be any sorrier than I am. I wish I could change, and if there was ever a man I'd do it for, it would be you. But you've seen how I am. I just don't want our last hours together to be spent arguing."

Philip took her hand and squeezed it tightly. "I don't either. We have tonight."

"And tomorrow," she murmured. But their flight was scheduled for the morning, and they'd be in the air a good portion of the day. Once they landed at Sea-Tac International Airport, Philip would catch a connecting flight a half hour later to Spokane. They would be separated by three hundred and fifteen miles that might as well have been three thousand.

"I have something for you," he announced casually, and pulled a small wrapped package from his coat pocket.

Astonished, Carla raised questioning eyes to Philip. "We must think alike. I've got something for you, too. I'd planned on giving it to you tomorrow. I didn't want you to forget me."

"There's little chance of that," he said with a wry twist of his mouth. "Go on, open it."

Eagerly, Carla tore off the ribbon and paper and was surprised to discover it was a jewelery box. Lifting the black velvet lid, she gasped in surprised pleasure. An exquisite turquoise necklace and matching earrings lay nestled in a bed of plush velvet. The ring he'd given her earlier matched the set. "Oh, Philip, you shouldn't have." Fresh tears misted her eyes, and she bit her bottom lip in an effort to forestall their flow. "They're beautiful. I'll treasure them always."

"Would you like me to help you put it on?"

"Please." She moved to the edge of the chair, turned and scooped up her hair with her forearm. Deftly, Philip placed the turquoise necklace against the hollow of her throat and fastened it in place. Carla managed the earrings on her own.

When she'd finished, she searched through her purse for a tissue to wipe away the tears that clouded her vision. She had to be crazy to walk away from the most wonderful man in the world. Crazy and stupid.

"Here comes Nancy and Eduardo," Philip announced, and stood as the introductions were being made.

The four sat together, and Carla was surprised to discover that Eduardo wasn't anything like she recalled. Her first impression had been all wrong. The Latin good looks were in evidence, but there was a natural shyness about him, a reserve that was far more appealing than his striking good looks. When he spoke English, his Spanish inflection was barely noticeable. Carla guessed that Eduardo had traveled extensively in the United States or had lived there. But more than anything else, Carla noted the way Eduardo watched Nancy. Each time his gaze swung to her friend, the dark eyes brightened and his masculine features would soften noticeably.

Conversation between the four flowed smoothly. When it came time to leave for dinner, Eduardo told them that the hotel's most expensive restaurant had a dining area designated especially for small private parties. The room resembled an intimate dining room, and had been reserved for them. A friend of his owned the hotel, Eduardo explained, and had given his permission for them to use this room. He led the way.

"It's lovely," Carla observed at first glance, impressed with the Aztec decor.

"I chose the menu myself," Eduardo explained. "I hope you will find it to your liking."

"I'm sure we will," Carla murmured. If the meal was anything like the room, this would be a dinner she'd remember all her life.

Eduardo continued by naming the dishes that they would be sampling. Carla understood little Spanish and appreciated it when Eduardo translated for her. "The food in Mexico is a combination of indigenous Indian dishes and Spanish cuisine with some Arabic and French influences."

Carla quit counting after six courses. Replete, she settled back in her chair, her hands cupping a wineglass. "And to think none of us would be here if you two men hadn't ordered a margarita that first night." Almost instantly Carla realized that she'd said the wrong thing. Nancy's eyes widened in warning, and Carla averted her gaze to the wineglass in her hand. Apparently, Nancy hadn't explained their game to Eduardo, and Carla had just stuck her foot in her mouth.

"I'm sorry?" Eduardo questioned, and a curious frown drew his thick brows together. "I don't understand."

"It's nothing," Nancy said quickly.

"Carla said something about Philip and me ordering margaritas the day we met. I'm confused."

"Really, it's nothing," Nancy insisted, a desperate edge to her voice.

An uneasy silence filled the room. "Please explain," Eduardo said stiffly. "A man doesn't like to be the only one not in on a joke."

"It wasn't a joke." Nancy avoided meeting Eduardo's probing gaze. "It's just that Carla and I never have any luck finding decent men, and we decided... Well, you see, we were sitting in the cocktail lounge and..." She tossed Carla a frantic glare. "You explain."

Carla's eyes rounded mutinously. "Nancy—I mean...we..." Good grief, she wasn't doing any better! Silently she implored Philip to take up the task.

To Carla's relief, Philip did exactly that, explaining at length in Spanish. Three pairs of eyes studied Eduardo, and it was easy to see that he was furious.

"And whose idea was this game?" His accent became thicker with every word.

"Mine," Nancy replied, accepting full responsibility. "But it wasn't like you think. I would never have—"

Pushing back his chair, Eduardo stood. "This has been an enjoyable time with my American friends, but I fear I have a business engagement and must cut our evening short."

Nancy stood up as well. "Eduardo, you can't leave now. We must . . ."

Philip leaned over to Carla.

"Let's leave these two alone to sort this out," he whispered in her ear, and they stood.

"How could I have said anything so stupid?" Carla moaned as they left the restaurant.

"You didn't know."

Philip's words did little to soothe her. "Didn't you see the look in Nancy's eyes? She'll never forgive me, and I don't blame her." Carla felt like weeping. "I've betrayed my best friend."

"Carla," Philip said, and placed an arm around her shoulder. "You can't blame yourself. Nancy should have said something to Eduardo before this."

"The bad part is that Eduardo honestly likes her, and I've ruined that. Oh, damn!" She kicked at a loose pebble. "I always did get a loose tongue when I drink too much wine."

Philip cleared his throat. "I hadn't noticed."

"And you're not helping things."

"Sorry." But his smile told her he wasn't. "You shouldn't worry. If Eduardo cares for Nancy, he'll give her the opportunity to explain."

"But I feel rotten."

"I know you do. Come on. Let's walk off some of that fantastic dinner." His arm tightened around her waist, and she propped her head against his shoulder.

The beach was possibly even more beautiful than it had been any night that week.

"Do you remember the first time we were here?" Philip asked, his voice low as he rubbed his chin along the top of her head.

Carla answered with a short shake of her head. "I remember thinking that you wanted to kiss me."

"I did."

"And at the time I was afraid you were the type of guy who would wait until the third date."

"Me?" He paused and pushed his glasses up the bridge of his nose. "And I was wondering what you'd do if I did make a pass."

A gentle breeze off the ocean carried Carla's soft laugh into the night. "No wonder you had a shocked look when we went swimming and I asked you to kiss me."

"I thought I'd died and gone to heaven."

The laughter faded and was replaced by a sadness born of the knowledge that within a matter of hours they would be separating. "This has been a wonderful week."

"The best."

Absently, Carla fingered the turquoise necklace. "I don't ever want this to end. This is heaven being here with you. Reality is only a few hours away."

"It doesn't have to end, you know." Philip stopped walking and turned her in his arms. His smoky gray eyes burned into hers. "I love you, Carla."

"Philip, please," she pleaded. "Don't."

"No, I'm going to say it. Believe me, I know all the arguments. One week is all we've had, and there are a thousand questions that still need to be answered. I want to get to know you, really know you. I want to meet your family and introduce you to mine.''

A bubble of pain and hysteria threatened to burst inside her. "You and my dad have a lot in common."

Philip ignored the sarcasm. "You're a beautiful, warm, intelligent woman."

"Don't forget conservative."

"And conservative," he added. "Have you ever thought how beautiful our children could be?"

"Philip, don't do this to me." She had thought about it. Blending her life with Philip's had been on her mind all afternoon. But no matter how appealing the imagery, Carla couldn't see past the police uniform and badge. "I... I think I should go back and check on Nancy. And I still have my packing to do."

Philip pinched his mouth tightly closed when he delivered her to the hotel room. "I'll see you in the morning," she promised, not meeting his gaze.

"In the morning," he repeated, but he didn't try to kiss her. Carla couldn't decide if she was grateful or not.

A muffled sound could be heard on the other side of the door. "Good night," she murmured miserably, and slipped inside her room.

Nancy was lying across the bed, her shoulders heaving as she wept. "Oh, Carla," she cried, and struggled to sit up. "Eduardo wouldn't even listen to me. He was barely polite."

Nancy and Carla looked at each other, and both burst into tears.

Chapter Six

The sun had barely crested the ocean, its golden strands etching their way across the morning beach, when Carla woke. Her roommate remained asleep as Carla slipped from the bed, quickly donning washed-out jeans and a warm sweatshirt. It wouldn't seem right to leave Mazatlán without one last walk along the water's edge.

Rushing down the concrete steps that led to the countless acres of white sand, Carla scanned the deserted area. Her spirits sank. This last stroll would have been perfect if Philip were here to share it with her.

Rolling up the jeans to her knees, she teased the oncoming tide with her bare feet. The water was warm and bubbly as it hit the shore. She vividly recalled the few times she'd swum in the surf with Philip. When the salt water had stung her eyes and momentarily blinded her, Philip had lifted her into his strong arms and carried her to shore.

With a wistful sigh, Carla strolled away from the water's edge, kicking up sand as she walked. Every memory of this vacation would be connected with Philip. She'd be a fool to think otherwise.

"Carla!"

Her heart swelled as she spun and waved her hand high above her head. Philip.

His shoulders were heaving by the time he ran the distance and joined her. "Morning." He reached for her and looked as if he meant to kiss her, then dropped his hands, apparently changing his mind.

"Morning. I was praying you'd be here."

"I thought I saw you by the pool."

The salty breeze carried her laughter. "I was there waiting for you to magically reappear."

"Poof. Here I am."

"Like magic," she whispered, and slipped her arm around his waist. They turned and continued strolling away from the hotel. The untouched morning beach meandered for miles in the distance.

"How's Nancy?"

Carla shrugged. "Asleep. But for how long, I don't know," she said as a reminder to them both that she couldn't stay long. "I guess Eduardo wouldn't let her explain that picking him up in the lounge never was a game. Not really."

"His attitude is difficult to understand, since Latin men are usually indulgent toward their women."

"Are you as indulgent toward your women?" Carla inquired with rounded, innocent eyes, determined to make this a happy conversation. She'd never be able to tell him all the things in her heart.

"I must be, or you would have shared my bed before now."

Forcing her gaze toward the sea, Carla struggled to maintain control of her fragile poise. "You sound mighty sure of yourself, Philip Garrison," she returned stiffly. If he'd said that for shock value, he'd succeeded. The evening in his parents' condo had caught her off guard. The atmosphere had been too intimate, and the wine had flown too freely.

"I don't think I'm being overconfident," Philip replied. "You wanted me as much as I did you. But whether you're willing to admit it is something else."

Carla understood what he was saying and flushed uncontrollably.

"What were you thinking when I called you just now?" Philip asked, breaking the uneasy silence that had settled over them. "I can't remember ever seeing you look more pensive."

"About Mexico and what a wonderful time I've had," she said, and smiled up at him. "That's mostly your doing. In my mind I'll never be able to separate the two."

"Me and Mazatlán?"

She answered with a short nod.

Her response didn't seem to please him. He glanced at his watch and applied a gentle pressure to the small of her back as he turned them around and headed for the hotel. "I'll take you back before Nancy wakes."

They didn't speak as they walked toward the El Cid. Then, Carla said somberly, "I was hoping you'd be here. My beach bag's up ahead. Your gift's inside." The hand-crafted marlin carved from rosewood had been expensive. Carla had seen Philip admire it the day they'd gone shopping at the arts and crafts center and had purchased the hand-rubbed wood sculpture for him while he had been talking to some Canadians.

Now her eyes shone with a happy-sad expression as Philip unwrapped the gift. He peeled back the paper and glanced at her wordlessly. Delight mingled with surprise as his eyes looked almost silver in the light of the morning sun.

"Thank you," he said simply.

"No," she replied, and swallowed against the hoarseness building in her throat. "Thank you. I'll never forget you, Philip, or this week we've shared. The reason for the marlin is so you won't forget me." She kissed him then, her hands sliding around his middle as her lips met his. It was meant to be a simple act of appreciation, but this kiss soon took on another, more intense significance. This was goodbye.

Philip's arms locked around her narrow waist, lifting her off her bare feet. Bittersweet memories merged with the pure hunger of their need. Mouths hardened against one another in a hungry, grinding demand. Their heads twisted slowly from side to side as the kiss continued and continued until Carla thought her lungs would burst. Incredibly, she couldn't give enough or take enough to satisfy the overwhelming passion consuming her resolve.

When they broke apart she was weak and panting. Her legs were incapable of holding her as she pressed her cheek to the hard wall of his chest and gloried in the thundering, erratic beat of his heart. Her shaking fingers toyed with the hair that curled along the back of his neck. But the comfort and security of his embrace was shattered when he spoke.

"Carla, I'm only going to ask you once. Can I see you once we're home?"

"Oh, Philip," she moaned, caught in the trap of indecision. He was forcing her to face the very question she dreaded most. Her lips felt dry, and she moistened them. She couldn't tell him 'yes,' although her heart was screaming for her to do exactly that. And 'no' was equally intolerable. Bright tears shimmered in her eyes as she stared up at him, silently pleading with him to understand that she couldn't say what he wanted to hear.

"Listen to me, Carla," he urged gently. "What we found in Mazatlán is rare. But two people can't know if they're in love after seven short days. We both need time to discover if what we've found is real." His hand smoothed the red curls behind her ear. "What do you say? Spokane isn't that far from Seattle, and meeting would be a simple matter of a phone call."

A tear broke from the building moisture in her blue eyes and streaked her face. "Oh, Philip, I'm such a coward." Her long nails made deep indentations in her palms, but she hardly noticed the pain.

"Say 'yes,'" he urged, his fingers gripping her shoulders.

Carla felt as if she were standing on the edge of the Grand Canyon looking down. She knew the pitfalls of loving Philip, and the terror of it gripped her, making speech impossible.

Trapped as she was, she couldn't agree or disagree. "I wish you wouldn't," she murmured finally.

The gray eyes she had come to adore hardened with an anger that was barely held in check. Philip dropped his hands to his side. "When you're through letting your fears and prejudices rule your life, let me know." Abruptly he turned, leaving her standing alone in the bright morning sunlight.

"Philip." Her feet kicked up sand as she raced after him. "We can talk more at the airport."

"No." He shook his head. "All along you've assumed I was booked on the same return flight as you. I won't be leaving for another two days."

"Oh." She was forced to continue running to keep up with his long strides. "Why didn't you say something?"

"Why? If you can't make up your mind by now, flying back together shouldn't make any difference."

He stopped and caressed the underside of her face. "Goodbye, Carla." His eyes were infinitely sad, and he looked as if he wanted to say something more, but changed his mind. Without another word he turned and left her.

Carla tried desperately to blink back the scalding tears that demanded release. Alone and hurting, she stood on the beach with the wind whipping at her from all directions.

"Phone. I think it's Cliff," Nancy announced on her way out of the kitchen.

Before Mexico the news would have been mildly thrilling. But Carla couldn't look at Cliff Hoffman and not be reminded of Philip. Not that the two men were anything alike. Cliff was the current heartthrob of half the medical staff at Highline Community Hospital. Carla had been flattered and excited when he'd started asking her out.

Unhooking her leg from the arm of the overstuffed chair, Carla set her book aside and moved into the kitchen, where the phone was mounted on the wall.

"Hello."

"Carla, it's Cliff."

"Hi." She hoped the enthusiasm in her voice didn't sound forced.

"How was Mexico?"

The question caught Carla off guard, and for one terrifying moment she couldn't breathe. "Fine."

"You don't sound enthusiastic. Don't tell me you got sick?"

"No...no, everything was fine." What a weak word "fine" was, Carla decided. It couldn't come close to describing the most gloriously wonderful, exciting vacation of her life. But she couldn't tell that to Cliff when she sounded on the verge of tears.

"I expected to hear from you by now. You've been back a week." She could hear an edge of disappointment in his voice, but suspected it was as phony as her enthusiasm. From the beginning of their nonrelationship, Cliff had let it be known she had plenty of competition. Philip had once asked her if there was anyone special waiting for her in Seattle. At the time, mentioning Cliff hadn't even crossed her mind.

"It's been hectic around here…unpacking and all." No excuse could have sounded so lame, and she smothered her giggles with a cough.

"I was thinking we should get together soon." Cliff left the invitation open-ended.

If he expected her to jump at the opportunity to spend time in his company, he was going to be disappointed. "Sure," she agreed without much enthusiasm.

"This weekend?"

Why not? she mused dejectedly. She wouldn't be doing anything by moping around the apartment, which was exactly what she and Nancy had been doing since their return. "That sounds good."

"Let's take in a movie Saturday night, then."

"Fine." There was that word again.

Five minutes later, Carla returned to the living room and her book.

"These arrived while you were on the phone." A huge bouquet of three dozen red roses captured her attention. Philip. Her heart soared. That crazy, wonderful man was wooing her with expensive flowers. It was exactly like him. She'd phone him and chastise him for being so extravagant, and then she'd tell him how miserable the last week had been without him.

Nancy sniffled and wiped the tears from her cheeks. "Eduardo sent them."

"Eduardo?"

"He sent the flowers in hopes that I'll forgive him for his behavior our last night in Mazatlán."

Carla felt like crying, too, but not for the same reasons as her roommate. "I'm really happy for you." At least one of them would be lifted from the doldrums.

"You might still hear from Philip."

"Sure," Carla said with an indifferent shrug. If anyone did anything to improve the situation between her and Philip, it would have to be she. And she couldn't, not when seeing him again would make it all the more difficult. As it was, he dominated her thoughts.

Fifteen minutes later the phone rang again. Carla's immediate reaction was to jump up and answer it, but Nancy was sitting closer to the telephone and for Carla to rush to it would be a dead give away. Although Carla pretended she was reading, her ears were finely tuned to the telephone conversation. When Nancy gave a small, happy cry, Carla's interest peaked. Eduardo, it had to be, especially since Nancy was exclaiming how much she loved the roses. She told him how sorry she was about the mix-up and how everything had changed since Mexico.

When her friend started whispering into the receiver, Carla decided it was time to make her exit. "I think I'll go visit Gramps," she said, reaching for her bulky knit sweater and her purse.

Nancy smiled in appreciation and gave a friendly wave as Carla walked toward the door.

The sky was overcast, and Carla swung a sweater over her shoulder as she walked out the front door. Summer didn't usually arrive in the Pacific Northwest until late July.

"See you later," Nancy called with a happy lilt of her voice.

Carla's Grandpa Benoit was her mother's father. He lived in a retirement center in south Seattle not far from Carla's apartment. Whereas Carla had always felt distant from her mother, she shared a special closeness with Gramps. Grandpa Benoit loved cards and games of any kind. From the time Carla could count, he had taught her cribbage, checkers and chess. The three essential C's, Gramps called them. it was because of Gramps that Carla had won the checkers championship through the King County Parks Department.

Pulling into the parking lot, Carla sat in her car for several minutes. If she showed up again today, Gramps's questions would only become more probing. From the day she'd returned to Seattle he'd guessed something had happened in Mexico. At first he hadn't pried; his questions had been general, as if her answers didn't much concern him. But Carla knew her grandfather too well to be tricked by that. Yesterday, when she'd stopped by on her way to work, they'd played a quick game of checkers, and Carla had lost on a stupid error.

"I guess that young man from Mexico must still be on your mind?" His eyes hadn't lifted from the playing board.

"What young man?"

"The one you haven't mentioned."

Carla ignored the comment. "Are you going to allow me a rematch or not?"

"Not." Still he didn't lift his gaze to hers. "Don't see much use in playing when your mind isn't on the game."

Carla bristled. She'd lost plenty of games to Gramps over the years, and it was unfair of him to comment on this one.

"Seems you should have lots of things you'd rather be doing than playing checkers with an old man anyways."

"Gramps!" Carla was shocked that he'd say something like that. "I love spending time with you. By now, I'd think you'd know that."

His veined hands lifted the round pieces one by one and replaced them in the tattered box. "Just seems to me a woman your age should be more interested in young men than her old Gramps."

Carla started picking up the red pieces. "His name's Philip. Does that satisfy you?"

The blue brightened on his ageless face. "He must be a special young man for you to miss him like this."

"He is special," Carla agreed.

Gramps hadn't asked anything more, and Carla hadn't voluntarily supplied additional information. But if she were to show up again today, Gramps wouldn't let her off as lightly.

Backing out of the parking space, Carla drove to a local Hallmark shop and spent an hour reading through cards. She selected two, more for the need to justify spending that much time in the store than from a desire for the cards.

That evening, as a gentle drizzle fell outside, Carla sat at the kitchen table and wrote to Philip. The letter was probably the most difficult of her life. Bunched-up sheets littered the tabletop. After two hours, she read her efforts with the nagging feeling that she'd said too much—and not nearly enough.

Dear Philip,

You told me to let you know when I was ready to let go of the fears that rule my life. I don't know that I'm entirely prepared to face you in full police uniform, but I know that I can't continue the way I have these last two weeks. Nothing's the same anymore, Philip. I lost a game of checkers yesterday, and Gramps said I shouldn't play if my mind isn't on the game. The only thing my mind's been on is you. The moon has your image marked on its face. The wind whispers your name. I can't look at the ocean without remembering our walks along the beach.

I'm not any less of a coward than I was in Mazatlán. But I don't know what to do anymore.

I used to be happy in Seattle. Now I'm miserable.

Even checkers doesn't help.

Once a long time ago I read that the longest journey begins with a single step. I'm making that first attempt. Be patient with me.

Carla

The letter went out in the next morning's mail. Since she didn't have Philip's address, Carla sent it to him in care of the Spokane Police Department. His return letter arrived four torturous days later.

Dear Carla,

My first reaction was to pick up the phone and call, but if I said everything that was going through my mind, I'd drive you straight to Alaska and I'm afraid you'd never stop running.

My partner must have thought I was crazy when the watch commander handed me your letter. I've read it through a thousand times and have been walking on air ever since. Do you mean it? I never dreamed I could take the place of checkers.

Carla, I don't know what's been going through that beautiful head of yours, but with every minute that passes I'm all the more convinced that I'm in love with you. I didn't want to blurt it out like this in a letter, but I'll go crazy if I hold it inside any longer. Get used to hearing it, love, because it feels too right to finally be able to say it.

You asked me to be patient. How can I be anything else when that first step you're taking is on the road that's leading you back to me?

Hurry and write. Your last letter is curling at the edges from so much handling.

I love you.

                                        Philip

P.S. I can tell I'm going to like your grandfather.

If Philip claimed to have read her letter a thousand times, then Carla must have doubled his record. Her response, a twelve-page epic, went out in the next day's mail.

Monday evening the phone rang. Nancy called Carla from the kitchen. "It's for you. Cliff, I think."

Carla was tempted to have her roommate tell him she wasn't home. Their date Saturday night had been a miserable failure. The movie had been a disappointment, and their conversation afterward had been awkward. But the problem wasn't Cliff, and Carla knew as much. Nothing was wrong with Cliff that substituting Philip wouldn't cure.

"Hello."

"Who the hell is Cliff?"

"Philip," Carla cried, and the swell of emotion filled her breast. "Is it really you? Oh, Philip, I've missed you so much." Holding the phone to her shoulder with her ear, she pressed her fingertips over her eyes. "Good grief, I think I'm going to cry."

"Who's Cliff?" he repeated, but the harsh anger had left his voice.

"No one important." How could he even think anyone meant half as much to her as he did? "We went out last Saturday night, and I think he was thoroughly pleased to be done with me. I'm rotten company at the moment." Her laugh was shaky. "It seems my thoughts are preoccupied of late."

"Mine, too. Jeff's ready to ask for a new partner. I haven't been worth a damn since I got back."

Carla stiffened, and her hand tightened over the receiver. If Philip was being careless, he could be stabbed again. Or worse.

"What's wrong? You've gone quiet all of a sudden."

"Oh, Philip, please be careful. If anything happened to you because you were thinking about me, I'd never forgive myself."

"Carla, I can take care of myself." The tone of his voice told her he was on the defensive.

Carla paused, remembering that he'd already been stabbed once. "I... I just don't want anything to happen to you."

"That makes two of us."

"I'm so glad you called," she said, and leaned against the countertop, suddenly needing its support. "I've never felt like this. Half the time I feel like I'm living my life by rote. Every day I rush home and pray there'll be something in the mail from you."

"I do, too," he admitted, his voice low and husky. "Listen, Carla, I've got two days off next Thursday and Friday. I'd like to come over."

"Philip, I'm scheduled in surgery both days."

"Can you get off?"

Carla lifted the hair from her forehead and closed her eyes in frustration. "I doubt it. This is vacation time and we're shorthanded as it is." Their mutual disappointment was clearly evident. "Don't be angry," Carla pleaded softly. "If it was up to me, I'd have you here in a minute. What about the weekends? Unless I'm on call I'll be free."

"But I won't."

"Right." She sucked in an unsteady breath. For a moment she'd forgotten that he didn't work regular hours. His life had to be arranged around his job. Even love came in a poor second to his responsibility to the force.

The awkward stillness fell between them a second time.

"Now you're angry?"

"No." The denial came automatically. "I understand a lot better than you realize. I can remember how rare it was to have Dad home on a weekend. Nothing has changed to make it any easier for you."

"You're wrong." Philip's voice dropped to a husky timbre. "Everything's changed. My life is involved with this incredible person who fills every waking thought and haunts my sleep."

"Oh, Philip."

"The worst part is that I get discouraged. You asked me to be patient and I promised I would be. I guess I'm looking for you to make leaps and bounds and not small steps."

Tears blurred her eyes, and her throat tightened. "I'm trying. Really trying."

For a long moment he didn't speak, but when he did, his voice was ragged. "Please, Carla, don't cry."

"I'm not," she lied, sniffling. "I wish I could be the kind of woman you want, but I can't."

"Carla—"

"Maybe it would be better if you quit wasting your time on me and found someone who can adjust to your life style." Her voice shook uncontrollably. "Someone who doesn't know the score...someone who doesn't understand what being a cop really means. Believe me, ignorance is bliss."

"Maybe I should," Philip said sharply. "There's not much to be said about a woman who prefers to live with her head buried in the sand."

Pain washed over her in waves, and she placed her hands over her eyes. All this time they'd been fooling themselves to think that either of them could change.

"I think you're right," she whispered in voice that was pitifully weak. "Goodbye, Philip."

He started to say something, but Carla didn't wait to listen. Very gently, very slowly, she replaced the receiver. She expected a flood of tears, but there were none—only a dry, aching pain that didn't ease. In some ways Carla doubted that it ever would.

Ten minutes later the phone rang again. Carla didn't answer it, knowing it was Philip. The phone was silent for the remainder of the evening.

Carla found two messages on the kitchen counter when she returned home from work the following afternoon. PHILIP PHONED. CLIFF DID, TOO.

Carla returned Cliff's call. They made arrangements to go to dinner Thursday night. Carla wasn't particularly interested in continuing her nonrelationship with Cliff. But not for the world would she let someone—anyone—accuse her of burying her head in the sand. That comment still hurt. Most girls should consider themselves lucky to be going out with Cliff. Obviously there was something about him she was missing. Thursday she'd make a determined effort to find out what it was.

Two days later a letter arrived from Philip, and Carla silently cursed herself for the way her heart leapt. She managed to make it all the way into the apartment, hang up her sweater and pour a cup of coffee before she ripped open the envelope.

Dearest Carla,

   I promised myself I wouldn't rush you, and then I do exactly that. Can you find it in your heart to forgive me? At least give me the chance to make it up to you.

   Be patient with me, too, my love.

                        Philip

Carla read the letter twenty times nonstop. Never had any two people been more mismatched. Never had any two people been more wrong for each other. But right or wrong, Carla couldn't ignore the fact that she'd never felt this strongly about a man. If this was what it meant to love, she hadn't realized what a painful emotion it could be.

Dear Officer Garrison,

   It's been brought to my attention that two people who obviously care deeply for one another are making themselves miserable. One has a tendency to expect overnight changes, and the other's got sand in her eyes from all those years of protecting her head. I'm writing to seek your advice on what can be done.

                        Carla

P.S. I'll be more patient with you if you're still

willing to stick it out with me. P.P.S. I've got a
date with Cliff Thursday night, but I promise not
to go out with him again. Maybe I should cancel
it.

Two days later Carla got a phone call from West-
ern Union.

"Telegram from Mr. Philip Garrison for Miss Carla
Walker."

She had never received a telegram before, and her
heart leapt to her throat as she searched frantically for
a pencil. "This is Carla. Will I need a piece of paper?"

"I don't think so. There are only two words: 'Break
date.'"

Chapter Seven

Early Thursday evening Carla rushed home from the hospital. "Did Philip call yet?" she asked breathlessly as she scurried inside the apartment.

Nancy looked up from her magazine, happiness lighting up her face. "Philip didn't, but Eduardo did. He's in Colorado on a business trip and wanted me to hop in the car and join him."

"You're joking?"

"No," she countered, "I'm totally serious. Obviously he had no idea how far Seattle is from Denver. We did have a nice talk though."

From the look on her roommate's face, Carla could see that the conversation with Eduardo had been very satisfying. Fleetingly, she wondered where the relationship would go from here. It was obvious the two were strongly attracted to each other. For Eduardo to have swallowed his pride and contacted Nancy, revealed how much he did care.

"So Philip hasn't phoned?" Disappointment settled over Carla. Everything was going so well with Nancy that she couldn't help feeling a small twinge of envy.

"Not yet. But it's a little early, don't you think?"

Carla had already kicked off her white loafers and was unbuttoning the front of her uniform. "It's not nearly early enough. I guess I can wait a few more minutes." In some ways, she'd been waiting a lifetime for Philip.

"What makes you so sure he's going to phone?" Nancy asked, following her down the hallway to the large bedroom they shared.

Carla laughed as she pulled the uniform over her head. "Easy. He'll want to know if I broke the date or not."

"And did you?"

"Of course. I'm not all that interested in Cliff."

Nancy released a sigh of relief. "I'm glad to hear that."

"Why?" Carla turned to her roommate as she slid pale blue cotton pants over her slender hips.

"Because he asked me out."

Carla was shocked. "Cliff did? Are you going?"

Nancy's eyes were evasive. "You don't mind, do you?"

Carla couldn't have been more shocked if Nancy suddenly had announced that she'd decided to date Dustin Hoffman. Her roommate had practically jumped for joy because Eduardo had phoned her, yet she was going out with Cliff. It didn't make sense.

"I don't mind in the least. But...but why would you want to? I thought you'd really fallen hard for Eduardo."

"I have," Nancy admitted freely, "maybe too hard. I want to know if what I feel is real or something I've blown out of proportion. We were only together for six days. And although I've been miserable without him ever since, I need to test my feelings. Eduardo's culture is different from ours, he thinks and reacts to things completely opposite of the way I do sometimes and that frightens me."

Nancy revealing she was frightened about anything was a shock. Of the two roommates, Nancy was by far the more stout-hearted. But she was the type who would be very sure before committing herself to Eduardo and once she did, it would be forever.

"But why date Cliff?" Carla wondered aloud.

"To be honest," she said a little shyly, lowering her eyes, "I've always been attracted to him, but you were seeing him and I'd never have gone out with him while you were."

"You like Cliff?"

Nancy nodded, indicating that she did. "But if it troubles you, I'll cancel the date."

"Don't," Carla said without the least hesitation. "As far as I'm concerned, Cliff is all yours."

The doorbell chimed and Nancy glanced at the front door. "That must be Cliff now. You're sure you don't mind?"

"Of course not. Enjoy yourselves, I'll talk to you later."

Too excited to bother eating dinner, Carla brought in a chair and placed it beside the phone. As an afterthought, she added a pencil, some paper and a tissue box in case she ended up crying again. Satisfied, she moved into the living room to watch the evening newscast.

When the phone rang, she was caught off guard and glanced at her wristwatch before leaping off the sofa.

"Hello," she answered in a low, seductive voice that was sure to send Philip's heartbeat racing.

There was a lengthy pause on the other end of the line. "Carla?"

"Mom." Embarrassed, Carla stiffened and rolled her eyes toward the kitchen ceiling. "Hi ... I was expecting someone else."

"Obviously. Is it someone I know?"

"No, his name's Philip Garrison. I met him in Mazatlán." She briefly related the story. "I thought he might be phoning tonight." Take the hint, Mom, and make this short, Carla pleaded silently.

"You and ... Philip must have hit it off for you to be answering the phone like a seductress."

"I like him very much," was all Carla would admit.

"Since you're so keen on this young man, when do your father and I get to meet him?"

Clenching a fist at her side, Carla struggled to hold on to her temper. She resented her mother for asking these questions, and she wanted to get off the phone in case Philip was trying to get through to her. "I don't know. Philip lives in Spokane."

"Spokane," her mother mused aloud. "Your father and I knew some people named Garrison. Delightful folks—"

"Mom," Carla interrupted, "would you mind if we talked later? I really do need to get off the phone."

"No, that'll be fine. I just wanted to know if you could come to dinner tomorrow night."

"Sure." At this point she would have agreed to anything. "What time?"

"Seven."

"I'll be there. Talk to you later."

"Goodbye, dear. And Carla, it might help if you're a little more subtle with . . . what's his name again?"

"Philip."

"Right. I'll see you tomorrow. And, Carla, do try to be demure."

"Yes, Mother, I'll try."

After hanging up, Carla took several calming breaths. She had never gotten on well with her mother. Over the years, Rachel Walker had admirably portrayed the role of a docile wife, but Carla had always thought of her as weak-willed: there were too many times when she'd witnessed the anger and hurt in her mother's expressive eyes. She had wanted to shout at both her parents. Her father should have known what his career was doing to the rest of the family. Her mother should have had the courage to speak up. Carla had tried at sixteen and had been silenced immediately, so she'd moved away from home as soon as possible, eager to leave a situation that made her more miserable every year. And now...here she was following in her mother's footsteps. A knot tightened in the pit of her stomach. Dear heavens, what was she getting herself into with loving Philip? Again and again she'd tried to tell herself that what they shared was different—that she and Philip were different from her parents. But their chances of avoiding the same problems her parents had dealt with were slim—likely nonexistent. With stiffening resolve, Carla vowed she would never live the type of life her mother had all these years. If that meant giving up Philip, then she'd do it. There wasn't a choice.

The phone rang again a half hour later. Carla stared at it as if it were a mad dog, her eyes wide with fear. Chills ran up and down her spine. Tears welled up in her eyes as she cupped a hand over her mouth to hold back the emotion. This was Philip phoning—the call she'd anticipated all day.

Trembling, she picked up her purse and walked out the door. A movie alone was preferable to listening to the phone ring every half hour. If she let Philip assume that she had gone out with Cliff, then maybe, just maybe, he'd give up on her and they could put an end to this misery. Her instincts had guided her well in the past. Now, more than at any other time in her life, she had to listen to her intuition—for both their sakes. Philip deserved a woman who would love him for his dedication to law and order and his commitment to protect and serve. He needed a wife who would learn the hazards of his profession a little at a time. Carla knew too much already.

Nancy wasn't back when Carla returned to the dark, lonely apartment. And within five minutes the phone rang. She ignored it. Coward, she taunted silently as she moved into the bedroom. But if she was behaving like a weakling, it shouldn't be this difficult. It wasn't right that it hurt this much.

Nancy was still asleep when Carla dressed for work the following morning. She penned her roommate a note and left it propped against the sugar bowl on the kitchen table: If Philip contacts you, please don't tell him I didn't go out with Cliff last night. I'll explain later. Also, don't bother with dinner. I'm going to my parents'. Am interested in hearing how things went with Cliff. Talk to you tonight.

Carla's first surgery was an emergency appendectomy, a teenage boy who was lucky to be alive. Carla had witnessed only a handful of deaths in the last couple of years. She didn't know how the rest of the staff dealt emotionally with the loss of a patient, but each one had affected her greatly.

When she had finished assisting with the appendectomy, she found a message waiting for her. She waited to read it until she was sitting down, savoring a cup of coffee in the cafeteria. Call Nancy, it read. A glance at the wall clock confirmed that there wouldn't be enough time to call until after lunch. When she phoned at one-thirty, however, there wasn't any answer, so Carla assumed it couldn't have been that urgent. She'd wait to talk to Nancy at home.

Three hours later Carla headed for the hospital parking lot, rubbing the ache in the small of her back to help relieve some of the tension accumulated from a long day on her feet. Dinner with her parents would only add to that tension. And eventually she would have to talk to Philip—he'd demand as much. But she didn't want to think about that now. Not when her back hurt and her head throbbed and she was facing an uncomfortable dinner with her parents.

Carla was soaking in a tub full of scented water when Nancy knocked on the bathroom door. "Carla."

"Hmm," she answered, savoring the luxurious feel of the warm, soothing water.

"I think you should get over to your grandfather's as soon as possible."

Carla sat up, sloshing water over the edge of the bathtub. "Why? What happened?"

"I can't explain now, I'll be leaving any minute. Cliff's on his way. He's taking me to the Seattle Center for the China Exhibit."

"Is anything wrong with Gramps?" Carla called out frantically. Already standing, she reaching for a thick towel to dry herself.

"No, nothing like that. It's a surprise."

"What about you and Cliff? Things must be working out if you're seeing him again." Carla could feel Nancy's hesitation on the other side of the bathroom door.

"They're working out, but not as I'd expected. I'm giving it a second chance to see if it's any better the second time."

"Oh?" Carla hoped that Nancy wasn't going to make her ask that she explain that.

"Cliff's all right, I guess."

Behind the closed door, Carla smiled smugly. That was how she felt about Cliff. He was fine, but he wasn't Philip, and now apparently he wasn't Eduardo either.

"Does Eduardo know? I mean did you tell him you were seeing another man?" Carla hated to think what would happen if he discovered Nancy was dating Cliff. Eduardo's male pride was bound to cause him to overreact.

"I . . . I told him yesterday."

"And?"

"Oh, he understands. In fact, he encouraged me to see Cliff again. I told him he should do the same thing and you know what he said? He said he didn't need to see another woman to know how he feels about me. He mentioned something about me flying to Mexico City to meet his family, but I didn't let him know one way or the other." As if regretting she'd revealed that much, Nancy added hastily, "Listen, Carla, I promise that you'll like your surprise. I'd hurry if I were you."

The doorbell sounded and was followed by a clicking sound that told Carla she wouldn't get any more information from her friend. A surprise! Presumably this was why Nancy had contacted her at the hospital.

Dressing casually in cotton pants and an antique white blouse with an eyelet collar, Carla hardly bothered with her hair. A quick application of lip gloss and a dab of perfume and she was out the door.

Her heart was hammering by the time she arrived at the retirement center. Her Swedish clogs clicked as she hurried inside, pushing open the double glass doors with both hands. She took the elevator to Gramps's room on the third floor, thinking it would be faster than running up the stairs.

Gramps's door was closed. Carla knocked loudly twice and let herself inside. "Gramps, Nancy..." The words died on her lips as her startled eyes clashed with Philip's. He was sitting opposite her grandfather, playing a game of checkers.

"Philip." She stood there, stunned. "What are you doing here?"

Gramps came to his feet, using his cane to help him stand. "Nancy brought your young man over to meet me."

"I asked her to," Philip added. "Your grandfather was someone I didn't want to miss meeting."

"Mighty fine young man you've got yourself," said Gramps, his blue eyes sparkling with approval.

"He could be saying that because he beat me in checkers," Philip explained, grinning.

Gramps's weathered face tightened to conceal a smile. "Leave an old man to his peace. Knowing my daughter, she'll have your hide if either of you is late for dinner."

"Dinner," Carla repeated with a panicked look.

"Yes, your mother was kind enough to include me in the invitation."

"My mother."

"Something's wrong with my hearing aid," Gramps complained, tapping lightly against his ear. "I'm hearing an echo."

Philip chuckled and cupped Carla's elbow. "Nice meeting you, Gramps," he said as he led the way out the door and into the hallway.

"Philip Garrison, what are you doing here?" Carla demanded, yanking her elbow free. Her hands rested defiantly on her hips. Damn, he looked good. His sandy-colored hair was combed to the side, and a thick lock fell carelessly across his wide brow. His appealing gray eyes were dark and intense as they met hers. To Carla he had never looked more compelling. Staying out of his arms was growing more difficult every minute.

"Are you trying to drive me crazy? Because you're sure as hell doing a fine job of it. Why wouldn't you answer the phone last night?"

"I . . . couldn't." She wouldn't lie outright, but she had no compunction about letting him believe she'd been out with Cliff.

"And while we're at it, you can explain this." He took Carla's note to Nancy from his pocket. "'Don't tell Philip I didn't go out with Cliff,'" he read with a sharp edge of bitterness lacing his voice. "It seems to me we've got some talking to do."

"Y-yes . . . yes, we do."

"Then let's go back to your place. At least there we can have some privacy." He flashed a look down the wide corridor.

They rode back to the apartment in silence.

"How'd you get here?" Carla asked shakily as she pulled into her assigned parking space.

"I flew in at noon. Nancy picked me up at the airport."

"When are you going back?"

His gaze cut into hers, and one thick brow arched arrogantly. "Can't wait to be rid of me, is that it?"

"No...yes...I don't know." She replied, her voice trembling.

With unsteady fingers she unlocked the apartment and stepped inside. Philip had come all this way because she hadn't had the courage to talk to him last night. She'd been foolish to believe he wouldn't find out why. A fine mist of tears momentarily blurred her vision as she moved inside the apartment.

"Would you like a cup of coffee?" she asked, hanging her purse over the inside doorknob of the coat closet.

Gently Philip settled a hand on each shoulder and turned her around so that he could study her. Carla's gaze fell to the floor.

"Carla, my love." Philip's voice was low, sensuously seductive. "You know what I want."

She did know. And she wanted it, too. "Oh, Philip," she groaned, and slippped her arms over his shoulders, linking her fingers behind his neck. "It's so good to see you."

His mouth claimed hers in a series of long, intoxicating kisses that left her weak and trembling. Philip was becoming a narcotic she had to have; his touch was addictive.

His hands roamed over her back, pulling her soft form against his muscular frame. A warmth spread through her limbs, and she turned her head when his lips explored the smooth curve of her shoulder and the hollow of her throat.

Taking a deep breath to keep the room from spinning, Carla pushed against his chest, leaving only a narrow space between them.

"How can you refuse to speak to me, deceive me by letting me think you'd gone out with this other guy, and then kiss me like that?" Philip demanded in a voice husky with emotion.

Melting against him, she explored his earlobe with her tongue as her fingertips caressed his clenched jaw. "I think I'm going crazy," she murmured at last. "I want you so much my heart's ready to pound right out of me."

His hand cupped her full breast, which swelled eagerly in his palm. "Then why?" he groaned against her ear. "Why are you running from me so hard I can barely keep up with you?"

"I'm so scared." Her low voice wavered. "I don't want to be like my mother."

"What's that got to do with anything?" He continued to nibble the side of her neck, making it impossible for her to think clearly.

"Everything," she cried desperately. "I'm not the right person for you."

"But I won't have anyone else."

"Philip, be reasonable."

"You're in my arms. I can't think straight." He bit gently at the edge of her lips. "Carla, I'm going crazy without you. I want you to marry me. I want to share my life with you, because God knows I can't take much more of this."

Carla's eyes shot open. "How can you talk about marriage?" she asked, struggling to break free of his hold.

"It's the normal process when two people feel as strongly about one another as we do."

"But I don't want to love you," she cried. Tears sparkled from the depths of her eyes. "When my husband leaves for work in the morning I don't want to worry about him risking his life on the streets of the city."

"Carla—"

"And when he comes home at night I don't want him to drag his job with him. I want a husband, not a hero—"

His mouth intercepted her words, muffling them until she surrendered to the mastery of his kiss, arousing her until she clung to him, seeking a deeper fulfillment. "Kissing me won't settle a thing," she murmured huskily, breaking free with her last reserves of strength.

"I know, but it keeps you from arguing."

"When you're holding me like this," she admitted shyly, "there's not much fight in me."

"Good. All I need to do for the next seventy years is keep you at my side. Agree, and I'll whisk you to a preacher so fast it'll make your head spin."

"You're incorrigible."

"I'm in love." His hands were linked at the small of her back and slipped over the rounded flesh of her buttocks, arching her upward to meet his descending mouth. The kiss was shattering.

"Can we talk now?" Every minute in his arms made it more difficult to think clearly.

"Okay, explain what happened yesterday," he said as they sat in the living room. "Why wouldn't you answer the phone last night?"

"I already told you why," she said, and exhaled slowly. "I don't want to be like my mother."

"Carla." Philip captured both her hands in his and kissed her knuckles. "That doesn't make any sense. You're who you are, and I'm me. Together we'll never be like anyone else."

Carla bowed her head, and her lashes fluttered until they closed completely. "Mom and I are a lot alike. You'll understand that when you meet her later. But she's weak and afraid and never says what she's really thinking. And Philip, I'm trying so hard to be different."

"That still doesn't explain why you wouldn't answer the phone."

Carla swallowed uncomfortably. "Mom called just before you did, and everything she said reminded me how unhappy she's been all these years."

"Ah," Philip said, and nodded thoughtfully. "And the note to Nancy?"

"I . . . I was thinking that if you assumed I was still dating Cliff, you'd give up on me."

He tucked his index finger under her chin and lifted her eyes to his. "I think there's something you'd better understand. I'm not giving up on you. Never. I love you, Carla."

"But loving someone doesn't make everything right," she argued. "We're different in so many ways."

"I don't see it like that. We complement each other. And although it seems like I'm the one who's asking you to make all the changes, I'm not. When we're married I promise that you and our family will be my first priority. Nothing will ever mean more to me than you."

"Oh, Philip." She felt herself weakening. "But it's more than that."

"I know, love." Slowly, deliberately, his eyes never leaving hers, he pulled her toward him. His mouth sought her lips, exploring their softness as if he would never get enough of the feel of her.

"Philip," she groaned, her voice ragged. "We have to leave now for my mother's."

"Your mother's," he repeated as if he needed something to bring him back from the brink.

"You'll be meeting my dad," she said softly, teasing his neck and ear with small, biting kisses.

Philip's hands captured her breasts, his thumbs circling her nipples until they were erect and hard. "And if he could see me now, I don't doubt that he'd arrest me."

"No doubt," she agreed with a deep sigh of longing.

"Mom and Dad, I'd like to introduce Philip Garrison." Carla stood just inside her parents' living room. "Philip, my mom and dad, Joe and Rachel Walker."

Joe stepped forward and shook Philip's hand. "Nice to meet you, Philip."

Carla felt the faint stirrings of pride. Her father, although graying, was in top physical condition. Over the years he hadn't lost the lean, military look of his younger days. Intuitively, Carla knew that in twenty years Philip wouldn't, either.

"It's a pleasure to have you join us," Rachel added warmly. "Carla said you live in Spokane."

"Yes, I flew in this afternoon."

The four of them sat in the large living room, and Philip immediately took Carla's hand in his. The action didn't go unnoticed by either of her parents. Rachel's blue eyes sought Carla's, and she gave her daughter a small wink, indicating that she approved of this young man. Maybe Carla should have been pleased, but she wasn't. Having her family like Philip would only complicate her feelings.

"And when will you be leaving?"

Carla was as interested in his answer as her parents.

"Tonight; I'd like to stay longer, but I'm on duty tomorrow morning."

"Carla said that you two met in Mazatlán."

"Yes, the first day she arrived." Philip looked at Carla, and his dark eyes flickered with barely concealed amusement.

Her eyes widened, silently warning him not to mention *how* they'd met. Then flustered, she cleared her throat and said, "Philip helped me out with my Spanish."

"You speak Spanish?" Joe asked, but his narrowed gaze studied Carla. Her father was too observant not to recognize that there was a lot going unsaid about her meeting with Philip. Fortunately he decided not to pursue the subject.

Rachel glanced at her gold wristwatch. "Excuse me a minute."

"Can I help, Mom?" Carla asked, and uncrossed her long legs.

"No, everything's ready, I just want to check the corn. Your father's barbecuing chicken tonight."

"You're in for a treat," Carla told Philip proudly. "I've been telling Dad for years that when he retires he should open a restaurant. He makes a barbecue sauce that's out of this world."

"It's an old family recipe that's been handed down for generations."

"He got it out of a Betty Crocker cookbook," Carla whispered, grinning. Then before her father could open his mouth, she stood. "I'll see what I can do to give Mom a hand." Although her mother had refused her offer, there was undoubtedly something she could do to help.

Rachel was taking a large bowl of potato salad from the refrigerator when Carla came through the swinging kitchen doors. "I like your young man," she announced without preamble.

Carla couldn't hold her mother's gaze. She should have been surprised; Rachel had disapproved of most of the men Carla dated. Her excuses were usually lame ones—this boy was careless, another boy was lazy. By the time Carla moved out, she had stopped introducing her dates to her parents. Somehow, though, she'd known her mother would approve of Philip.

"He's clean-cut, polite and he has a nice smile."

Carla bit into a sweet pickle from the relish tray. "And his eyes are the most incredible gray. Did you notice that?" Naturally they wouldn't discuss any of the important aspects of her relationship with Philip.

"You two make a nice couple."

"Thank you," Carla answered with a hint of impatience. She opened the silverware drawer and counted out forks and spoons. "I'll set the table."

Philip was holding a beer, watching her father baste the chicken with a thick coating of pungent sauce, when Carla joined them on the sunny patio. He slipped an arm over her shoulder. His thumb made lazy, sensuous forays at the base of her neck.

Annoyed, she shrugged her shoulder and Philip dropped his hand to her waist. She didn't want him to make this kind of blanket statement to her family about their relationship. *He* was serious about her, but she had yet to deal with her feelings about him. When she stepped free of his hold, Philip firmly but gently cupped her shoulder.

"Philip," she groaned in an irritated whisper. "Please don't."

His eyes sparkled as he leaned toward her. "I told your father outright that I'm going to marry you."

"You didn't!" she cried in angry frustration.

Joe turned aside from the barbecue. "Hand me a spoon, would you, Carla?" he requested, and his gaze followed her as she moved to the picnic table and brought back a spoon. "Problems, Princess?"

"No." She shook her head, the red curls bouncing with the action. "I'm just sorry that Philip made it look like we're more serious than we are."

"He was rather forthright in his feelings."

Carla swallowed. "I know."

"But aren't you sure?"

"I won't marry a cop." Years of self-discipline masked any physical reaction from her father.

"I can't say I blame you for that," he said after a long moment. Some of the brightness faded from his eyes as he concentrated on his task.

"I love you, Dad, you know that. But I won't love the life Mom has."

With practised skill he turned the chicken over with a pair of tongs. "She's never complained."

"Oh, Dad," Carla said with a rush of inner sadness. She respected and admired her father and had never thought of him as oblivious of the stress his career had placed on their family. "Are you really so blind?"

His mouth tightened, and the look he gave her was piercing. "I said she's never complained. It takes a special kind of woman to love a man like me."

Carla lifted her gaze to Philip, who was examining the meticulously kept flower beds, and her father's words echoed in her mind. Carla didn't know if she could ever be that special kind of woman.

Rachel appeared at the sliding glass door. "Carla, would you help me carry out the salads?"

"Sure, Mom." Carla followed her mother into the kitchen.

Rachel stuck a serving spoon in the potato salad, handed it to Carla and turned away. "Philip mentioned that he had to be back tomorrow because he's on duty. You did say he was a doctor, didn't you?" Her voice was unnaturally high, and her hands were busily working around the sink.

"No, Mom." She'd wondered how long it would take for her mother to pick up on that. "Philip's a police officer."

A glass fell against the aluminium sink and shattered into little pieces. Rachel ignored it as she turned, her face suddenly waxen. "Oh, Carla, no."

Chapter Eight

Your flight will be boarding in a minute." Carla stood stiffly in the wide corridor of the airport concourse. The lump in her throat was making it hard for her to talk. The crazy part was that she didn't want Philip to leave and at the same time she couldn't bear to have him stay.

The meal with her parents had been an ordeal. As she had suspected, Philip and her father had gotten on like soul mates. They were alike in more ways than Carla had first suspected. Their personalities, ideas and thoughts meshed as if they were father and son.

Rachel had remained subdued during most of the meal. Later, when Carla had helped clear the picnic table and load the dishwasher, a strained tension had existed between them. Her mother had asked a few polite questions about Philip, which Carla had answered in the same cordial tone.

"I don't think it would be a good idea for you to become too serious with this young man," Rachel said as they were finishing. Her casual attitude didn't fool Carla.

Fleetingly, Carla wondered what reason her mother would give. Philip wasn't the careless type, and even the most casual observer could see he wasn't lazy. She was bound to say everything but what was really on her mind.

"Why not?" Carla implored. "I thought you said you liked him."

"I do," Rachel replied quickly in a defensive tone. "But he's too much like your father, and I'll love that man to my death." The poignant softness of Rachel's voice cracked the thin wall that stood between mother and daughter.

"And you," Rachel continued with a wry grin, "are too much like me: vulnerable, sensitive, tender-hearted. Our emotions run high, and when we love, we love with a fervor. Philip could hurt you, Princess."

Her mother so rarely called her by that affectionate term that Carla lifted her head in surprise.

"There are plenty of men in this world who will make life a thousand times easier for you than someone involved in law enforcement."

"But you married Dad," Carla argued, studying her mother intently. This was as close as they had ever come to an open conversation.

"Your father joined the force after we were married."

"I . . . I didn't know that."

"Something else you may not know is that Joe and I separated for a time before you were born."

Shocked, Carla's mouth dropped open. "You and Dad?"

Rachel busily wiped off the kitchen counter, then rinsed out the rag under the running faucet. "There are certain qualities a policeman's wife should have. I...I've never been the right woman—" She stopped in midsentence as Philip and Joe sauntered into the kitchen.

Mother and daughter had been unable to finish the conversation, but Carla had felt a closeness with her mother she had never experienced. She realized now that they had always been too much alike to appreciate each other.

"Carla?"

Philip's voice brought her back to the present, and to the reality of his leaving.

"You're looking thoughtful." His fingers caressed the gentle slope of her neck, trailing down her shoulder. "I expect a kiss goodbye, one that will hold me until I see you again."

A smile briefly touched Carla's eyes. "I don't think that kind of kissing is allowed in public places."

"I don't care." His voice was low and husky as he ran his hands up and down the length of her silken arms. "Seeing each other again has only made things worse, hasn't it?"

"No," she denied instantly. "I think it's been good for us both."

"Good and bad," he growled, and the frustration and longing in his eyes deepened. "Good, because holding you lessens the ache I feel when we're apart." His hands gripped the back of her collar, bringing her closer into his embrace. "And bad, because I don't know how much longer it'll be before I hold you again."

Their gazes met and held, and Carla felt as if she were suffocating. His eyes, steel gray and narrowed, slowed the torment within him, and Carla realized hers were filled with doubt. Her lips started quivering, and she pressed them tightly together.

A flight attendant stepped to the microphone and advised passengers bound for Spokane and Boise to have their boarding passes ready.

Philip's hands tightened on Carla's blouse, and he dipped his head forward so that their foreheads touched. "I hate this."

Her arms slid around his waist, and she pressed her face to his shirt. "I do, too." Her voice was scratchy and unnaturally high as she swallowed hard, determined not to let Philip see her cry. "You should go," she said, and gave him a brave smile.

"Not until the last minute. Not until I have to." His voice wasn't any more controlled than her own. "Carla" —he breathed in deeply—"I want to do everything right for you. You need me to be patient and wait; then I'll do that."

"Oh . . . Ph . . . Philip." His name was lost in a sob. "How can you love me? I'm so wrong for you."

"No one has ever been more right," he insisted, his words muffled against her hair. "I love you, and someday we'll have beautiful redheaded children."

"With warm gray eyes."

"Tall," he added.

"Naturally," she said, and offered him a shaky smile.

"Does this mean that you've reconsidered and will marry me? Because let me warn you: if it does, I'll make the arrangements tomorrow."

She couldn't answer him. Something deep and dark in her soul wouldn't allow her to speak. Instead she blinked her eyes in an effort to hold back the emotion that threatened to overtake her.

Disappointment, regret, pain and several other emotions Carla couldn't name played across Philip's face.

"Soon?" he asked in a whisper.

Tears that refused to be forestalled any longer filled her eyes, and she forced a smile. "Maybe."

"That's good enough for now. Just make it soon, my love. Make it very soon."

The final announcement came from the flight attendant, and Philip tossed an impatient glare over his shoulder. His kiss was short, but ardent. As he turned and hurried onto the boarding ramp, Carla pressed four fingers to her lips and closed her eyes, savoring the feel of him for a few precious moments more.

She didn't leave the terminal until the plane was out of sight and her tears had dried. Her spirits were at an all-time low as she headed to the airport parking lot, fighting back questions that tormented her from all sides.

Philip's letter arrived in Saturday's mail.

My dearest love,

It's been only a few hours since I left you in Seattle. I couldn't sleep, and it's too late to phone. As I flew back tonight I couldn't drop the picture of your tear-streaked face from my mind. Knowing I'm the one who caused those tears only makes leaving you more difficult.

This week is hectic, but I'll phone you Tuesday night. I'm involved with three other friends from the force in a canoe race—don't laugh. Ever hear of the Great Soap Lake Canoe Race? Well, yours truly is captain of the motley crew. We're planning to arrive in Soap Lake Friday afternoon. The race begins early Saturday morning. The others have their own cheering squad. I have only you. Tell me you'll come. I want to introduce you to my friends and their wives. And for all the trouble I've been giving Jeff Griffin, my partner, since Mexico, he claims he has a right to meet you. Let me warn you now that you shouldn't believe everything he says. Jeff likes to tease, and believe me he's had a lot to kid me about the last few weeks. I want you to talk to Jeff's wife when you come. Sylvia is pregnant with their first child. I know you'll like her. Please tell me you'll be there.

This is torment, Carla. I can feel your kiss on my lips, and the scent of your perfume lingers, so all that I need to do is close my eyes and imagine you're with me. And, my love, don't ever doubt I want you with me. I'm praying that this feeling can hold me until Friday.

I love you.

Philip

Carla read his letter again and again, savoring each word, each line. Several times she ran her index finger back and forth over his declaration of love. Philip sounded so sure of things. Sure that they were right for each other. Sure that she could put her insecurities behind her. Sure that she would eventually marry him.

And Carla felt none of it. Every day the list of pros and cons grew longer. Philip, like her father, was an idealist. Carla wasn't convinced that being in love made everything a rose garden.

As for his invitation to have her come and root for him in the canoe race, Carla was sure that the real reason was so she could meet his friends. And she didn't need to be told that policemen usually socialized with other policemen. Her parents had few friends outside the force; the same undoubtedly held true for Philip. Friday was only a few days away and finding someone willing to trade work days would be difficult with half the staff scheduled for vacation time. It was a convenient excuse until she made up her mind what to do.

"Have you decided what you're going to tell him?" Nancy asked Tuesday evening as she carted her luggage into the living room. After her last date with Cliff, Nancy had returned convinced she knew what she was feeling for Eduardo. When he'd pressed the invitation for her to meet his family she hadn't hesitated.

"No," Carla answered dismally. "I'm afraid that I'll be dragged into his life little by little until we're married and I don't even know what happened."

"I think Philip's counting on that."

"I know." Carla nibbled on her bottom lip. Philip would be phoning this evening, and she still didn't know what she was going to tell him. If she told him outright that she wouldn't come, he'd accuse her of burying her head in the sand again. And he'd be right. But if she did agree, Carla realized that things would never be quite the same again. He had come to Seattle and invaded her world. He'd played checkers with Gramps and had dinner with her parents. She didn't feel safe anymore. Inch by inch he was entwining their lives until it would be impossible for her to escape.

A happy, excited Nancy had left for Mexico by the time Philip phoned. Carla stared at the phone for five long rings before she had the courage to pick up the receiver.

"Hello." As hard as she tried, she couldn't disguise her unhappiness.

"Carla, what's wrong?" She wanted to cry at the gentle concern that coated his voice. "You aren't coming," he said before she could answer.

"I . . . I don't know. Friday's a busy day at the hospital, and finding a replacement—"

"You don't want to come," he interrupted impatiently.

"It's not that." Carla leaned her hip against the counter and closed her eyes in defeat. "It's too soon for this sort of thing. I don't think I'm ready."

"For a canoe race!" he barked.

Carla could feel his anger reverberate through the telephone lines. "You said you'd give me time and then you immediately start pushing at me. You're not playing fair, Philip Garrison. Don't force me into something I'm not ready to deal with yet."

"You mean to say you can't handle a social outing with my friends?"

"I don't know," she cried.

An unnatural, tension-filled silence followed. Carla struggled for some assurance to give him and found none. Maybe Philip was seeking the same. A full minute passed and neither spoke, yet neither was willing to break off the connection.

Carla heard Philip take a deep breath. "All right, I won't push you. I said I'd be patient. When you decide if you're going to come, phone me." From the tone of his voice, she knew that he was hurt and discouraged. "I'll be out most of the week—practising with the rest of the team." Apparently he wanted her to realize why he wouldn't be available. "If you can't reach me, I'll be waiting at the B and B Root Beer stand in Soap Lake from seven to nine Friday night. It's on the main road going through town. You can't miss it. If you don't come, I'll understand."

"I'll call you before then." The lump in her throat made her voice sound tight.

"I'd appreciate that."

Again there was silence, and again it was obvious neither of them wished to end the conversation.

"I . . . I have some good news about Nancy," Carla said at last. "She's flying to Mexico City to meet Eduardo's family. From the way things have been progressing I wouldn't be surprised if Nancy returned wearing an engagement ring."

"You could be too." Philip told her in a tight voice and Carla regretted having said anything. It'd been a mistake to bring up the subject of Nancy and Eduardo in the light of their own circumstances.

"I know."

"But you're not ready? Right?"

"Right," Carla returned miserably.

The strained silence returned until Philip finally spoke, his voice devoid of anger. "Eduardo's a good man."

So are you, Carla mentally added.

"So you think Nancy may marry Eduardo."

"It wouldn't surprise me," Carla said, forcing an air of cheerfulness into her voice. "Nancy's a lucky girl." The second the words were out, Carla desperately wanted to take them back. "Philip," she said contritely, and swallowed. "I didn't mean that the way it sounded."

"The problem is, I believe it's exactly what you mean. I'm not a good looking, Latin American who's going to impress your friends." His words were as cold as a blast of wind from the Arctic.

"Philip, you're everything I want in a man except . . ."

"Except...I've heard it all before. Goodbye, Carla, if I see you Friday, that's fine. If not, that's fine too."

The phone clicked in her ear and droned for several moments until Carla replaced the receiver. The entire conversation had gone poorly. She'd hoped to at least start off in a lighter mood, and then explain her hesitancy about meeting him for the weekend. But she'd only succeeded in angering Philip. And he was furious. She knew him well enough to realize this type of cold wrath was rare. Most things rolled off him like rain water on a well-waxed car. Only the important matters in his life could provoke this kind of deep anger. And Carla was important.

She still hadn't decided what to do by the time she joined her grandfather after work on Thursday for their regular game of checkers. Carla hoped he wouldn't try to influence her to go. She'd taken Gramps out to dinner Sunday afternoon, and he had done little else but talk about what a nice young man Philip was. By the end of the day, Carla had never been more pleased to take him back to the retirement home. She prayed today wouldn't be a repeat of last Sunday.

"Afternoon, Gramps," she greeted him as she stepped into his small apartment.

Gramps had already set up the board and was sitting in his comfortable chair waiting for her. "The more I think about that young man of yours, the more I like him."

"Philip's not my young man," she corrected more tersely than she had intended. Carla had suspected this would happen when Philip met her family. Gramps and her dad had joined forces with Philip—it was unfair!

"'The lady doth protest too much'—Shakespeare."

Carla laughed, her first real laugh in two days. She and Gramps played this game of quotes occasionally. "'To be is to do'—Socrates," she tossed back lightly as she pulled out the rocking chair opposite him and sat down.

Gramps's eyes brightened and he stroked his chin, deep in contemplation. "'To do is to be'—Sartre." He nodded curtly to Carla, and the set of his mouth said he doubted that she could match him.

"'Do be do be do'—Sinatra," she said, and giggled. For the first time in recent memory she'd outwitted her grandfather. Soon Gramps's deep chuckles joined her own, and his face shone with pride. "I'm going to miss you, girl."

"Miss me?" She opened the game of checkers by making the first move.

"When you and Philip marry you'll be moving to Spokane to live with him."

Miffed, Carla pressed her lips tightly together and removed her hand from the faded board. "Did he tell you that?"

"Nope." Gramps made his return move.

With her fingers laced together in her lap, Carla paused and looked up from the checkers. "Then what makes you think I'm going to marry him?"

"You'd be a damn fool not to. The boy clearly loves you, and even more obvious is the way you feel about him."

Carla returned her gaze to the checker pieces, but her mind wasn't on the game. "He's a cop, Gramps."

"So? Seems to me your daddy's been a fine officer of the law for twenty-odd years."

"And Mom's been miserable every minute of those twenty-odd years."

"Your mother's a worrier. It's in her blood," Gramps countered sharply. "She'd have fretted about your dad if he was the local dogcatcher."

"But I'm afraid of being like Mom," Carla declared vehemently. "I can't see myself pacing the floors alone at night when Philip's called on a case, or when he isn't and just goes away for a while to settle things in his head. Don't you have any idea of how much time Mom spends alone? She's by herself when she needs Dad. But he's out there" —she pointed to the world outside the apartment window—"making the city a better place to live and forgetting about his own wife and family." Her voice was high and faltering as she spewed out her doubts in one giant breath. "Gramps, I'm afraid. I'm afraid of loving the wrong man." Her fists were tightly clenched, and her nails cut painfully into her skin.

"And you think Philip is the wrong man?"

"I don't know anymore, Gramps. I'm so confused."

His gnarled hand reached across the card table and patted her arm. "And so in love."

Talking out her fears with Gramps had a releasing effect on her, Carla realized as she walked around the lonely apartment hours later. Only a few days ago

Philip had been sitting on that couch, holding her as if he'd choose death rather than let her go.

Her gaze was drawn to the telephone. She'd promised to call him by now and let him know if she was coming. Her heartbeat accelerated at the thought of hearing his voice. With trembling resolve, she picked up the telephone, punched out the unlisted number he'd given her and waited for the electronic bleeps to connect their lines.

Philip answered on the first ring with a disgruntled "Yes?"

"Do you always answer your phone like you want to bite off someone's head?" Just hearing his voice, unwelcome and surly as it was, had her heart pounding erratically.

A long pause followed. "Carla?"

"The one and only," she answered. Her voice throbbed with happiness. She'd pictured him lying back in an easy chair and relaxing. Now she envisioned him sitting up abruptly and rolling to his feet in disbelief. The imagery produced a deep smile of satisfaction.

"You called!" This time there was no disguising his incredulity.

"I said I would," she murmured softly.

"You've decided about the canoe race?"

"Yes."

"And?"

"First, I need to know if you're wearing your glasses."

"Good grief, Carla, what's that got to do with anything?"

"Do you have your glasses on or don't you?" she demanded arrogantly.

"Why?"

Carla was learning that he could be just as stubborn as she. "Because what I'm about to say may steam them up, so I suggest you remove them."

Washington was known as the Evergreen State, but there was little evidence of any green in the eastern portion of the state—and none at all in the sagebrush, desert-like area in which Carla was traveling. Divided by the Cascade mountain range, Washington had a wet side and a dry side. In Seattle, summer and winters were less extreme—for example, althought it was already mid-July, there had been only a handful of days above seventy-five degrees.

Carla shifted in the driver's seat of her compact car, hoping to find a more comfortable position. She'd been on the road for almost four hours and was miserably hot. Her bare thighs stuck to the vinyl seat of her car, and rivulets of perspiration trickled down the small valley between her breasts. Even Mazatlán hadn't seemed as hot.

Exiting off the interstate freeway at George, Carla gassed up her car at Martha's Inn and paused to read over the map a second time. Within an hour or so she would be meeting Philip. They'd been apart only six days, yet it felt more like six years. Carla didn't know how she was going to endure any long separations.

As he'd said he would, Philip was sitting at a picnic table in front of the B and B Drive-In. Carla savored the sight of him and did a quick self-inspection in her rearview mirror. Instantly, she was sorry she hadn't stopped at a service station outside of town to freshen her makeup.

As she pulled into the drive-in's parking lot, she noticed that Philip had spotted her and was heading for her car. Carla's throat was dry, and she couldn't think of a thing to say.

"Hi." Philip opened the driver's side and gave her his hand, his face searching hers all the while as if he couldn't quite believe she wasn't an apparition. The hand gripping hers tightened. "How was your trip?"

"Uneventful," was all Carla could manage.

Lightly, Philip brought her into his arms and brushed her cheek with his lips. Their eyes met as they parted, and still he didn't smile. "You really came," he said hoarsely.

She answered with a short nod. Philip had known without her fully explaining what her coming meant. The doubts, her determination to fight this relationship, were slowly dissolving. And coming here to meet his friends was a major step on her part.

"Jeff and Sylvia will be by in a few minutes." He led her to a picnic table. "Sit down and I'll get you something cool to drink."

"I can use that." Now that she was outside the car, the heat was even more sweltering.

Philip returned with two cold mugs of root beer. He set them on the table and sat opposite her. "I can't believe this. My heart's beating so fast I feel like an adolescent out on his first date."

"I feel the same way." She lowered her gaze to the root beer. Her fingers curled around the mug handle, and she took her first long drink. "I noticed in your letter you said that you wanted me to talk to Sylvia."

Philip's hand reached for hers. "I think you two will have a lot in common."

"Does she feel about cops the way I do?" Carla asked tentatively.

"No." His voice was gently gruff. "But you're about the same age."

"Didn't you say she was pregnant with their first child?"

"Very." He said it with an odd little smile. "You'll be beautiful pregnant."

Carla could feel herself blushing. "Honestly, Philip," she murmured, her eyes looking troubled. "I wish you wouldn't say things like that."

"Why not? Last night after we finished talking I was so happy that I lay in bed thinking I could run ten miles and not even feel it. But I didn't run. Instead I lay there and closed my eyes, picturing what our lives would be like five years from now."

"And?" She was angry with herself for going along with this fantasy, but she couldn't help herself.

"You were in the kitchen cooking dinner when I walked in the back door. A little redheaded boy was playing at your feet, banging pots and pans with a wooden spoon. When you turned to me, I saw that you were pregnant. I swear, Carla, you were so beautiful I went weak. My heart stopped beating and my knees felt like putty. I don't think anything's ever affected me like that. I've never made any pretense about wanting you, and I'm not going to start now."

Carla busied herself by running her finger along the rim of her mug, and when she lifted her gaze, their eyes met. "That's beautiful," she said, and was shocked at how low her voice was. The closeness she felt with him at that moment was beyond anything she had ever known. But she wished he wouldn't say such things to her. It only made her more miserable.

Silence fell between them, but Philip seemed content to watch her. Her hands trembled as she lifted the mug for another long drink. "Philip," she moaned, finding his continued scrutiny uncomfortable, "please stop looking at me like that. You're embarrassing me."

Immediately he dropped his gaze. "I didn't mean to. It seems I do everything wrong where you're concerned. I thought I'd play it cool today when you arrived. And the minute I saw you every nonchalant greeting I'd practised died on my lips."

"Mine too," she confessed shakily.

"I'm still having trouble believing that you came."

"We both need to thank Gramps for that."

"I think we should name our first son after him."

Carla shook her head. "He'd never forgive us for naming a boy Otis."

"All right, we'll name him after your dad."

"He'd like that." Good heavens, the sun must have some effect on her mind. Here they were discussing the names of their children, and Carla wasn't even convinced she should marry Philip!

"Jeff and Sylvia are here," he announced, and his expression became sober. Carla turned and noticed a sky-blue, half-ton pickup kick up gravel as it pulled into the parking lot.

A lanky fellow with a thick patch of dark hair jumped down from the driver's seat and hurried around to help his obviously pregnant wife.

Sylvia, a petite blonde with warm blue eyes, pressed a hand to the small of her back as she ambled toward them. Carla guessed that Jeff's wife must be seven or eight months pregnant.

"Hi, you must be Carla." Jeff held out his hand, not waiting for an introduction.

"Hi. You must be Jeff."

Sylvia offered her a gracious smile. "I'm glad you could make it."

"The whole team's ecstatic she could make it. Philip hasn't been worth a damn since he got back from Mexico. I certainly hope you're going to put this poor guy out of his misery and marry him."

Carla's startled eyes clashed with Philip's. This was exactly what she'd feared would happen. She didn't want to have to answer these kinds of questions. They were bad enough coming from Philip and Gramps.

"I . . . I'm not sure what I'm going to do," she answered stiffly, her eyes damning Philip.

Chapter Nine

The warm sun had disappeared beyond the horizon, and the sunbaked land cheerfully welcomed the cool breath of evening. The flickering flames of a campfire licked at the remaining pieces of dry wood.

Sylvia and Carla were the last to remain by the dying fire. The other women were busy tucking their little ones into bed, and the sound of their whispers and hushed giggles filled the still evening air. Carla and Sylvia glanced at each other and grinned. Next year Sylvia would be joining the other young mothers. And next year Carla... She closed her eyes and shook her head. She didn't know what she'd be doing.

Jeff, Philip and the rest of the ten-man relay team were meeting to plan their strategy for the coming race. An air of excitement drifted through the campgrounds. The Great Soap Lake Canoe Race had dominated the conversation all afternoon. This was the first year the Spokane Police Department was competing, and their cheering squad held high expectations. For the last couple of years, the eighteen-and-a-half-mile course had been won by a two-man marathon team in the amazing time of two hours and thirty minutes. Philip's teammates seemed to think that ten men in top physical condition could easily outmaneuver two. The most incredible fact, Carla thought, was that every team that had ever entered this outrageous competition had finished. "Carla?" Sylvia's voice broke into her reverie, and she looked up.

"Hmm?"

"Jeff didn't mean to put you on the spot this afternoon—about marrying Philip, I mean," Sylvia said shyly. "It's just that we all like him so much."

"I...like Philip, too." The toe of Carla's sandal traced lazy patterns in the dirt. "In fact, I love him."

"You didn't need to tell me that. It's obvious."

A sad smile played at the edges of Carla's mouth. She liked Sylvia. She'd discovered that she liked all of Philip's friends. They had welcomed her without hesitation and accepted her as a part of their group, going out of their way to include her in the conversation and activities. One of Philip's friends had worked in Seattle for a short time and remembered Carla's father. Perhaps that was the reason she was accepted so quickly, but Carla didn't like to think so.

"The natural thing to do when two people love one another is to get married," Sylvia suggested softly.

"Not always," Carla answered with an emotional tremor in her voice. "Oftentimes there are...

extenuating circumstances. My father's a police-man."

"I heard." Sylvia slipped her arms into the sleeves of the thin sweater draped over her shoulders and leaned back against the folding chair. "I can under-stand your hesitancy. Being a policeman isn't the kind of work I would have chosen for Jeff. There are too many worries, too many potential dangers that affect both our lives. But Jeff's career is an important part of who he is. It was a package deal, and I've had to learn to accept it. Each police wife must come to grips with it sooner or later."

"Philip's got to be the most patient man in the world to put up with me."

"He loves you." Sylvia smiled. "I remember the first week after Philip returned from Mexico. Jeff complained every night." She paused and laughed softly. "A lovesick Philip took us all by surprise. We just didn't expect him to be so human. He's been as solid as a rock, and we were shocked to discover he's as vulnerable as the rest of us."

"He was in love with a stewardess a few years back. Did you ever meet Nicole?"

"No." Sylvia shook her head slowly. "That was before I married Jeff. But I can remember him men-tioning how hard Philip took it when they split up. I think Jeff's worried the same thing is going to hap-pen again."

Rather than offer reassurances she didn't have, Carla said, "Philip's like that. Everything is done full measure."

"Everything," Sylvia agreed.

"Nicole was a fool to let him go." Carla paused and sucked in her breath, realizing what she'd just said. She'd be a fool to allow her fears and inhibitions to ruin her life. Yet something within her, some unresolved part of herself, couldn't accept what Philip was. The other wives had come to terms, appreciating their men for what they were. Carla hadn't honored Philip's commitment to his career, just as her mother had never been able to fully respect her father's dedication to his. The thought was so profound that it caused Carla to straighten up. Maybe for the first time in her life she needed to talk with her mother.

"Would you like some help out of that chair, Mommy?" Jeff asked as he stepped behind his wife and lovingly rested his hand on her shoulder.

"Next time, I'm going to let him be the one to get pregnant," Sylvia teased, and extended her hand, accepting her husband's offer of assistance.

With their arms wrapped around each other, Jeff and Sylvia headed toward their tent.

"Night, Carla," Sylvia called back with a yawn. "I'll see you in the morning."

"Night."

"Are you tired?" Philip asked as he took the chair Sylvia had vacated.

"Not yet." Not when she could spend a few minutes alone with Philip. Not when they could sit undisturbed in the quiet of the night and talk. There were so many things she wanted to tell him. But in the peaceful solitude by the campfire, none of them seemed important.

"It's a beautiful night," he murmured as he leaned back and stared up at the sky. "In fact, tonight reminds me of Mexico and this incredibly lovely woman I once held in my arms."

"If I close my eyes, I can almost hear the surf against the shore," Carla responded, joining his game. "And if I try, really try, I can picture this incredibly wonderful man I met in Mexico sitting across from me."

Philip's chuckle was deep and warm. "How hard do you need to try?"

"It's not so difficult, really."

"I should hope not." Philip smiled and moved his chair so that they were sitting side by side. When he sat back down and reached for her hand, Carla glanced at him. His strong face was profiled in the moonlight, his look deep and thoughtful.

"Have you got your strategy all worked out, Oh master of the canoe race?" she asked lightly. His pensive look troubled her. She didn't want anything to ruin these few minutes alone together; this wasn't the time to discuss her doubts or find the answers to nagging questions.

"Pretty much." He grimaced and quickly disguised a look of pain.

"Philip, what's wrong?" Her voice was unnaturally high with concern. "You're not feeling well, are you?" Immediately she knelt at his side and touched his brow, which was cool and revealed no sign of a fever.

"It's nothing." He tried to dispel her worry with a wide grin. "Nerves, I think. I'm always this way before a race."

Returning to her chair, Carla nodded. "I had the lead in a play when I was in the eighth grade, and I was deathly sick before the first performance. I know what you mean."

"Have you and Sylvia decided where you're going to position yourselves to cheer us on?"

Apparently Philip didn't want to talk about his nerves, this Carla understood and could sympathize. "At the finish line. Sylvia isn't in any condition to go running from lake to lake with the rest of the team. So we've decided to plant ourselves there and wait for our dedicated heroes to bring in the trophy."

"You may have a long wait," Philip said wryly and grimaced again.

Carla decided not to comment this time, but she was concerned. "Five lakes, Philip. Are you guys honestly going to canoe across five lakes?"

"We're going to paddle like crazy across each one, then lift the boat over our heads and run like madmen to the checkpoint. From there the next two-man team will take the canoe and the whole process will start again."

"Which lakes?" Carla had heard them mentioned only fleetingly.

"Park, Blue, Alkaline, Lenore and Soap."

"I think you're all a little nuts."

"We must be," Philip agreed soberly. "But to be honest, I'd swim, hike, canoe and run a lot farther than a few miles for an excuse to have you with me."

He raised her fingers to his lips and kissed the back of her hand.

He studied her in the moonlight, and, feeling wretched, Carla lowered her eyes to the smoldering fire. "I don't know how you can love me," she murmured.

"Patience has its own rewards."

"I do love you." But a declaration of love, she knew, was only a small part of what he wanted from her.

"I know." He stood and offered her his arm. "I think we should both turn in. Tomorrow's going to be a full day." His voice was bland, almost impersonal, but his tone was at odds with the look in his eyes. Carla would have sworn he was hiding something from her and it was a whole lot more than nerves.

Philip's kiss outside her tent was brief, as if he were more preoccupied with the race than he was with having her near. It could be nerves, but they'd only seen each other twice since Mexico and she'd thought he'd do a whole lot more than pecking her cheek when it came time to say goodnight. A hand on her hip, Carla tipped her head to one side and flashed him a confused glance as he turned toward the tent he was sharing with Jeff and Sylvia. Carla didn't know what was troubling Philip, but she'd bet hard cash it had nothing to do with her or the race. But whatever it was, he wasn't going to tell her. That hurt; it seemed to prove that Philip didn't feel he could discuss his problems with her. He wanted her to share his life, but there was a part of himself he would always hold back. As her father had from her mother.

Carla didn't know there were this many people in all Eastern Washington. The start of the race was jam-packed with participants, friends, casual observers and cheering fans. Some of the contestants wore identifying uniforms that would distinguish themselves as being looney enough to participate in such a laughable race.

Everyone had been laughing and joking before the race, but when the gun went off, the competition began in earnest; each team was determined to win.

Jumping up and down with the others and clapping as hard as she could, Carla was caught up in the swirl of craziness that seemed to have engulfed the entire city of Soap Lake.

Three hours later, when Philip and Jeff crossed the finish line, placing a respectable fifth, Carla and Sylvia had cheered and laughed themselves weak.

Dramatically throwing themselves down on the grass, both men lay staring at the cloudless blue sky, panting.

Jeff spoke first. "Next year," he managed breathlessly, "we'll go after the trophy."

Sitting around the picnic table at the campgrounds later that afternoon, Philip positioned himself by Carla's side and casually draped his arm over her shoulder. "Do you think we should compete again next year?"

Carla lowered her hot dog to the plate. "It'd be a shame not to. You were only twenty minutes off the best time, and with a little practice you're bound to improve. Don't you agree?"

"On one condition. That you promise to be on my cheering squad again next year." His eyes searched hers, seeming to need reassurance.

Confidently, Carla placed her hand on his. "You got it." The sun beamed off the gold band of her watch, and Carla noticed the time and groaned.

"What's the matter?"

"I've got to leave."

"Now?"

Sadly, she shook her head. "Soon. In order to have Friday afternoon free, I traded days with another girl who's on call tomorrow."

"Which means?" His eyes narrowed.

"Which means I have to be back tonight by midnight in case there's an emergency."

Standing, Philip tossed his paper plate in the garbage can. Carla dumped the remainder of her lunch away and followed Philip to a large oak tree, where he stood, staring at the ground.

"It was hardly worth your while to make the trip. I'm surprised you came."

"I'm glad I did. I enjoyed meeting your friends, especially Sylvia and Jeff."

He pursed his lips, and Carla studied him suspiciously. He looked as if he wanted to argue and she couldn't understand why. Planting herself in front of him, her legs braced slightly apart, she stared at him until he met her gaze. "It's not going to work, you know."

He frowned. "What's not going to work?"

"Starting an argument. I refuse to react to your anger. I wish I could stay. If it was up to me, I would.

But circumstances being what they are, I've got to leave this afternoon." She paused and drew a long breath. "Now. Will you walk me to the tent and spend the next few minutes saying goodbye to me properly, or are you going to stand here and pout?"

Philip bristled. "I never pout."

"Good." She smiled and reached for his hand. "Then let's escape for a few minutes of privacy before someone comes looking for us."

The sun was setting, whisking back the splashes of warm, golden rays, by the time Carla pulled into her apartment parking space. After emerging from the car, she stretched, raising her arms high above her head and yawning. The trip back had been leisurely and had taken the better part of six hours. Philip had promised to phone Monday after work. That brooding, troubled look had returned when he'd kissed her goodbye. Carla didn't know what was bothering him, but she guessed that it had nothing to do with her. Already he was acting like her father, afraid to tell her something he knew could upset her. If she was going to consider being his wife, she didn't want him treading lightly around information she had a right to know. She'd ask him about it Monday night.

Sunday afternoon, her telephone beeper attached to her purse, Carla drove to her parents' house.

"Hi, Mom," she said as she let herself in the front door. Rachel Walker was sitting on the worn sofa, crocheting a sweater.

"Who's this one for?" Carla asked as she sat across from her mother, admiring the collage of colored yarn. Rachel was constantly doing something—idle hands led to boredom, she had always said. She was a perfectionist housekeeper, and now that Carla and her brother had left home, she busied herself with craft projects.

"Julianne," her mother replied without a pause between stitches, her fingers moving with a skill that was amazing. "She'll need a warm sweater this fall for first grade. She's six now, you know."

"Yes." Both her nieces had always been special to Carla, and she'd missed them terribly since her brother and his wife had moved to Oregon.

"Where's Dad?"

Briefly a hurt look rushed across her mother's face. "He's playing on the men's softball team again this year." The Seattle Police Department had several teams, and Carla's father loved to participate, but her mother had never gone to watch him play, preferring to stay at home. What Joe did outside the house was his business, because it involved the police force—and Rachel had never had anything to do with the force.

"Actually I'm glad Dad isn't here, because I'd like to talk to you alone."

"To me?" Momentarily, Rachel glanced up from her handiwork.

"I'm in love with Philip Garrison," Carla announced, and closed her eyes, preparing for the backlash that was sure to follow.

"I think I already knew that," her mother replied calmly. "In fact, your father and I were just talking about the two of you."

"And?"

"We agreed that you and Philip will do fine. What I said to you the other night isn't altogether valid. We are alike, Carla, in many ways, but in others we're completely different."

Carla marveled at the way her mother could talk so seriously with her and at the same time keep perfect pace with her crocheting.

"Joe pointed out that your personality is stronger than I've given you credit for. You're not afraid to say what you feel or to speak out against injustice. Your work at the hospital proves that..." Rachel paused, and tears rolled down her pale face. Taking a shuddering breath, she bit her bottom lip.

Carla moved out of the chair and kneeled at her mother's side. Rachel tossed her yarn aside and leaned forward to hug her daughter as she hadn't since Carla was a child. "I would have chosen another man for you, Princess. But I can't hold against Philip the very things that make me love your father. Be happy, baby. Be happy."

"I love you, Mom," Carla murmured, tears clouding her vision. She'd never thought she'd feel this close to her mother. Philip had done that for her. He had given her the parent she had never thought she'd understand—the closeness every daughter yearns to share with her mother.

Wiping the tears from her face, Carla laughed and said, "It's not every day your only daughter decides to get married. Could we do something together? Just you and me."

Leaning back in the cushioned sofa, Rachel reached for a tissue and blew her nose. "What do you want to do?"

"Can we go to Dad's softball game?"

For a second Rachel looked stunned. But gradually a smile formed at the edges of her mouth. "I've been waiting twenty years for an excuse to do just that."

Monday afternoon, on her way home from the hospital, Carla stopped off to visit Gramps, but she stayed just long enough for a single game of checkers and to tell him she'd made a decision about Philip.

"So you've come to your senses and decided you're going to marry him?"

"If he'll have me."

"No worry there," Gramps said with a chuckle. "The problem, as I see it, is if you're ready to be the right person for a man like Philip."

Carla didn't hesitate. "I know I am. Philip is a policeman, and I should know what that means. After all, I've been a policeman's daughter all my life."

His eyes beamed with pride as he slowly shook his head. "I see you've come to terms with that. Now I pray that you'll be as good a wife as your mother has been all these years."

"I hope I can, too," Carla added soberly.

The phone was ringing when she let herself into the apartment. Carla dumped her purse on the kitchen table and rushed to answer it.

"Hello."

"Carla. Thank God I got you. Where have you been? This is Jeff, Philip's partner."

Carla felt the blood rush from her face. Jeff would be phoning her only if something had happened to Philip. Her knees went weak, and she leaned heavily against the counter. "What is it?"

"Philip's in the hospital. I think you should get here as soon as possible. I checked with Air West, and there's a flight leaving Seattle in an hour. If you can be on it, I'll pick you up in the patrol car and take you directly to him."

Chapter Ten

W hat happened?'' Somehow Carla managed to get the words past the bubble of hysteria that threatened to overtake her.

''We were on patrol and . . . It was my fault. Damn, I should have known what was happening. With all the medical training I've had, I can't believe I didn't know what was going on. But I got him to the hospital in record time. Listen, Carla, I can't explain everything now. Just get here. Philip asked for you when he came out of surgery. I want to tell him that you're coming.''

''Yes . . . of course, I'm on my way now. And Jeff.'' She brushed the stinging tears from her eyes. ''Thanks for letting me know.''

Unable to move, even after she'd replaced the phone in its cradle, Carla felt an almost tangible fear move through her body. Her senses reeled with it. Her mouth was dry, her hands were clammy, her knees felt weak. Even the rhythmic beating of her heart slowed. It seemed unfair that once she had reconciled herself to who and what Philip was, her newfound confidence should be severly tested this way. With a resolve born of love, Carla had thought she could face anything. Now she realized how wrong she was. She would never come to terms with losing Philip.

By rote, her fingers trembling, she punched out her parents' phone number. "Mom," she cried, not waiting for a greeting, "Philip's been shot." Carla heard her mother's soft gasp and fought her own rising panic. "He's just out of surgery and I'm flying to be with him. Call the hospital and explain that I won't be in. And let Gramps know."

"When's your flight."

Carla ran her hands through her hair. "In an hour.... I've got to make reservations with Air West and pack."

"I'll call the airport for you. Your father will be there in ten minutes to drive you. Don't worry, Princess, Philip will be fine." Her mother hadn't any more information than Carla, but the gentle reassurance gave her the courage to think clearly.

Yanking clothes off the hanger, Carla stuffed them in an overnight case. After adding her toothbrush, curling iron and a comb, she slammed the lid closed. She'd be fine if only she could stop shaking. Pausing, she forced herself to take several deep, calming breaths. The shock of Jeff's call prevented tears, but she knew those would come later.

The doorbell rang, and Carla rushed across the living room to open the door.

"You ready?" Her father looked as pale as she did, Carla realized, but she knew he was far too disciplined to display his emotion openly.

She gave an abrupt nod, and Joe took the small suitcase out of her hand and cupped her elbow as they hurried down the flight of stairs to the apartment parking lot. During the ten-minute drive to Sea-Tac International, Carla could feel her father's concerned scrutiny.

"Are you going to be all right, Princess? Do you want your mother with you?"

No, I'm fine," she said, and with a sad smile amended,"I think I'm fine. If anything happens to Philip, I don't know that I'll ever get over it.''

"Cross that bridge when you come to it," he advised. "And phone as soon as you know his condition."

"I will," she promised.

Jeff was nervously pacing the tiled airport floor when Carla spotted him just minutes after stepping off the plane. Without hesitation she ran to him and gripped his forearm. "How's Philip?" Her eyes pleaded with him to tell her everything was fine.

"There weren't any complications. But apparently I misunderstood him. He had said that he *didn't* want you to know."

"Didn't want me to know?" she echoed incredulously. If that bullet didn't kill him, she would. Philip was lying on a hospital bed wanting to protect her from the unpleasant aspects of his occupation. It infuriated her, and at the same time she felt an over-powering surge of love.

"Just before I left, the doctors told me it would be several hours before he wakes."

Carla weighed Jeff's words carefully. "Take me to the hospital. I want to be there when he does."

A smile cracked the tight line of Jeff's mouth. "As the lady requests. Tell him the decision was yours and I'm not responsible."

"I'll tell him," she said and winked.

"Great." He looked at his watch. "I'm afraid I can't take you to the hospital personally; I'm still on duty. But another friend of ours will get you there safely. If you like, I can take your things and drop them off at Philip's condo."

"Yes . . . that'll be fine."

Jeff introduced Bill Bower, a ruddy-faced officer Carla didn't recognize from the previous weekend. Bill nodded politely, and after saying goodbye to Jeff, the two of them headed for Bill's car.

"Can you tell me what happened?" she asked Bill when they were on the freeway. During the flight she had prepared herself to hear the details of what exactly had gone wrong. In some ways Carla realized that she didn't want to know. It wasn't important as long as Philip was alive and well. There would be time for explanations later when Philip could make them himself. But knowing that he would make light of the incident, she'd hoped to get a fuller version of the story on the way to the hospital.

"I wasn't there," Bill stared matter-of-factly, "so I don't know how it happened. But apparently Philip was in tremendous pain, and Jeff may have saved his life by getting him to the hospital as quickly as he did.''

Carla paled at the thought of Philip in agony. He'd be the type to suffer nobly. Her lips felt dry, and she moistened them.

The stoic-faced offer must have caught her involuntary action. ''I wouldn't worry. Philip's healthy and strong. But he's bound to be in a foul mood, so don't pay any mind to what he says.''

''No, I won't,'' she replied with a brave smile.

The hospital smelled fainty of antiseptic. Carla was admitted into Philip's room without question, which surprised her. Seeing him lying against the white sheets, tubes coming out of his arms, nearly undid her. She sank gratefully into the chair beside his bed.

''The doctor will be in later, if you have any questions,'' the efficient nurse explained.

''I'll be leaving now,'' added Bill. ''If you need anything, don't hesitate to call. Jeff will be back later tonight.''

''Thanks, Bill.''

''All the thanks I want is an invitation to the wedding.''

''It's yours.'' She tried to smile, but the effort was painful.

Still wrapped in the warm comfort of sleep, Philip did little more than roll his head from one side to the other during the next two hours. Content just to be close to him, Carla did little more than hold his fingers in hers and press her cheek to the back of his hand.

''Carla?''

Forcing herself to smile, Carla raised her head and met Philip's gaze.

"Is it really you, or is this some befuddling dream?"

"If I kiss you, you'll know for sure." Gently she moved to the head of his bed and leaned forward to press her lips to his. Philip's hand found her hair, and he wove his fingers through its rusty curls.

"Oh, Philip, are you going to be all right?" she moaned, burying her face in the side of his neck.

"Stay a while longer, and I'll prove it," he whispered against her temple.

He lifted his gaze to hers, and the intense look in those steel-gray eyes caught her breath. A muscle worked in his lean jaw as his gaze roamed possessively over her face. "I didn't want Jeff to contact you."

"I know, but I'm here now and nothing's going to make me leave." Her hand clasped his as she took the seat beside the bed.

"What did Jeff say when he phoned? He has a high sense of theatrics, you realize."

"You warned me about that once before. He said that you'd just come out of surgery and had asked for me."

"What I asked was that he not contact you. I didn't want you worrying."

"Philip Garrison, if you think you can keep something like getting shot from me" —she tried to disguise the hurt in her voice—"you've got a second think coming, because I can assure you, wild canoe racers wouldn't keep me away from you at a time like this."

"Shot?" His breath quickened as he raised his head slightly to study her. "Jeff told you I was shot? I'll kill him."

"Well, good heavens, something like a gunshot wound is a little difficult to keep from me. Just how were you planning to tell me about it? 'Carla, darling'" she mimicked in a deep rumbling voice, "'I guess I should explain that I got scratched while on duty today. I'll be in the hospital a week or so, but it's nothing to worry about'"

"Carla..." His voice was a husky growl. "If I told you I'd been shot, paranoia would overtake you so quickly that I'd never catch you, you'd be running so fast."

"It's a high opinion you've got of me, isn't it?" she asked in a shaky voice. "You're missing the point. I did learn what happened, and I'm here, because it's exactly where I want to be."

"Only because Jeff made it sound as if I were on my deathbed."

"He said you asked for me—that's all."

"And I hadn't."

Sitting became intolerable, and she stood, pacing the floor with her arms gently wrapped around her to ward off the chill in his voice.

"As it is, you've wasted a trip. There won't be any deathbed scene. I was never in any danger from a gunshot wound. I had my appendix out."

Carla pivoted sharply and her mouth dropped open. "Your appendix out?"

"If you need proof, lift the sheet and see for yourself."

She ignored the heavy sarcasm lacing his voice. "Then why did Jeff—" What kind of fool game was Philip's friend playing anyway? Did he feel he needed to fabricate stories to convince her to come?

"That's exactly what I intend to find out."

Silence hovered over them like a heavy thundercloud.

"I don't mean to be rude, but I'm not exactly in the mood for company, Carla."

Stinging tears filled her eyes, and she blinked in a futile effort to forestall their flow. She'd thought he'd been shot and all the while it was his appendix. To her humiliation, she sniffled and her soft breath became a hiccuping sob. Frantically, she searched for her purse, needing to get out of the room before she humiliated herself further.

"Carla. Dammit," he groaned in frustration. "I didn't mean that. I'm sorry."

"That's all right," she mumbled shakily, wiping the tears from her pale cheeks. A kaleidoscope of emotions whirled through her—shock, relief, hurt, anger, joy. "I understand."

"This is exactly what I didn't want. If it had been up to me, you wouldn't even have known I was in the hospital. I don't want you worrying about me."

"You didn't even want me to know you were in the hospital?" Carla closed her eyes as waves of pain washed over her. Carla didn't want to think about the life they'd have if Philip insisted on shielding her from anything unpleasant. She wondered how he'd feel if the tables were turned. Damn she was going to get Jeff for this. She'd arrived expecting something far worse and he'd let her believe it!

"I may be out of line here, but didn't you ask me to marry you not long ago?" she demanded.

Philip looked at her blankly. "What's that got to do with anything?"

"Doesn't a wife or a fiancée or even the woman in your life have a right to know certain things?"

His hand covered his weary eyes. "Do you mind very much if we discuss this at another time? Go back to Seattle, Carla. I'll call you sometime this week and we can discuss it then."

Placing four fingers at her temple, she executed a crisp military salute. "Aye aye, Comandant."

Carla couldn't tell whether the sound Philip made was a chuckle or a snort, and she didn't stay long enough in his room to find out.

Luckily, Jeff was due to arrive at the hospital within a half hour. Her anger mounted by the time Philip's partner arrived. The minute he appeared she stood, prepared for battle.

"That was a rotten trick you pulled," she declared with clenched teeth.

"Trick?" Jeff looked stunned. "I didn't pull any trick."

"You told me Philip had been shot."

Jeff looked all the more taken aback. "I didn't."

"You implied as much," she returned, barely managing to keep her voice even.

"How could you have thought he'd been shot? Especially since he was feeling so crummy during the canoe race. Saturday night someone even suggested it

could be his appendix and..." Jeff swallowed, looking chagrined. "That's right, you left early. Phil was
feeling even crummier later and I think we all should
have known what was wrong. Listen, I apologize, I
thought you knew. You must have been frantic. I
wouldn't have frightened you had—"

"It's all right," Carla accepted his apology with a
wry grin. Obviously she had read more into his com-
ments then he had intended. The misunderstanding
hadn't been intentional.

"I'd better explain to Philip," Jeff said with a
thoughtful look. "He's probably mad as hops."

"It's best to let the beast rest for now. If you want
you can explain later."

One glance at Carla was apparently enough to convince him that Carla knew what she was talking about.
The ride through Spokane seemed to take forever and
when Jeff stopped at a traffic light, Carla couldn't
hold back a giggle.

"What's so funny?" Jeff glanced at her curiously.

"I don't know...just my thoughts, I guess. I assumed that someone as wonderful as Philip would be
a good patient. I thought he'd be the type of man to
suffer silently...and he's terrible. Just terrible."

"Give him a day or two," Jeff advised good-
humoredly. "He'll come around."

Philip's condominium was located in the heart of
the city near the Spokane River. "Here are the keys to
his car," Jeff said, handing them to her after unlock-
ing the front door. They stood just inside the entry-
way. "Bill dropped it off on his way home tonight.
Listen..." Jeff paused and ran his hand along the side

of his short-cropped hair. "Sylvia called and said she was feeling strange. I don't know what that means, but I think I should head home. I have this irrational fear that the baby is going to come into this world without me coaching, and I'd hate to think that all those classes would go to waste. Call if you need anything, all right?"

"Sure. Go on, and give Sylvia my best."

"I will. Thanks."

Jeff was out the door, and Carla turned to interrupt Philip's orderly life even more by invading his home. Maybe he was right; maybe she should take her things and head back to Seattle. No, she wouldn't do that. Things between them had to be settled now.

The first thing that caught Carla's attention was the hand-carved marlin that she'd given Philip. He'd set it on the fireplace mantel. A photo of them together in Mexico sat on his dresser. Carla was smiling into the camera as the wind whipped up her soft russet curls. Philip's head was turned and his eyes were on her. There was so much love in his expression that Carla breathed a soft sigh as she examined the framed photo.

Her letters to him were stacked on the kitchen table. Each one had been read so many times that the edges had begun to curl. Carla took one look and recognized again that there wasn't any man on earth who would love her as much as Philip. And more important, there would never be anyone she could love as much.

After a reassuring phone call to her parents, she took a long shower and slept fitfully.

She waited until noon the next day before venturing outside the condominium. Driving Philip's car to the hospital proved to be eventful. Twice she got lost, but with the friendly help of a local service-station attendant, she finally located the hospital.

A nurse on Philip's floor gave her a suspicious look as she walked down the wide corridor carrying a guitar.

One loud knock against his door was all the warning she gave.

"Carla."

She suspected it was relief she heard in his voice, but she didn't pause to question him. Instead she pulled out the chair beside his bed, sat at an angle on the cushion and strummed one discordant chord. With that she proceeded to serenade him in the only song she knew in Spanish.

He started to laugh but quickly grimaced and tried to contain his amusement. "Why are you singing to me the A, B, C's?"

"It's the only Spanish song I know all the way through. However, if you'd like to hear parts of 'Mary Had a Little Lamb,' I'll be happy to comply."

Extending a hand to her, he shook his head. "The only thing I want is you."

"That's a different tune than you were singing yesterday."

"Yesterday I was an unreasonable boor." He pulled her closer to his side. "I'm glad you're here. Today I promise to be a much better patient."

"Once we're married I suspect I'll have ways of helping you out of those irrational moods."

The room went quiet as Philip's eyes sought hers. "Once we're married."

"You did ask me, and you damn well better not have changed your mind, because I've already given my two-week notice at the hospital."

"Carla." His gray eyes reflected an intensity she had rarely witnessed. "Do you mean it?"

"I've never been more serious in my life. But I won't have you holding out on me. If I'm going to be your wife, I expect you to trust me enough not to try to shield me from whatever comes our way. I'm stronger than I look, Philip Garrison."

"Far stronger," he agreed as his hand slipped around her waist. "You've already convinced me of that. I love you, Carla Walker—soon to be Carla Garrison."

Tenderness surged through her as she slipped her arms over his shoulders. "But not near soon enough," she said with a sigh of longing as her mouth eagerly sought his.

AMERICAN TRIBUTE

Where a man's dreams count
for more than his parentage...

*Look for these upcoming titles
under the Special Edition
American Tribute banner.*

LOVE'S HAUNTING REFRAIN
Ada Steward #289—February 1986
For thirty years a deep dark secret kept them
apart—King Stockton made his millions while
his wife, Amelia, held everything together.
Now could they tell their secret, could they
admit their love?

THIS LONG WINTER PAST
Jeanne Stephens #295—March 1986
Detective Cody Wakefield checked out
Assistant District Attorney Liann McDowell,
but only in his leisure time. For it was the
danger of Cody's job that caused Liann to
shy away.

AM-TRIB-1

Silhouette Special Edition

AMERICAN TRIBUTE

AMERICAN TRIBUTE

RIGHT BEHIND THE RAIN
Elaine Camp #301—April 1986
The difficulty of coping with her brother's
death brought reporter Raleigh Torrence
to the office of Evan Younger, a police
psychologist. He helped her to deal with
her feelings and emotions, including love.

CHEROKEE FIRE
Gena Dalton #307—May 1986
It was Sabrina Dante's silver spoon that
Cherokee cowboy Jarod Redfeather couldn't
trust. The two lovers came from opposite
worlds, but Jarod's Indian heritage taught
them to overcome their differences.

NOBODY'S FOOL
Renee Roszel #313—June 1986
Everyone bet that Martin Dante and Cara
Torrence would get together. But Martin
wasn't putting any money down, and Cara
was out to prove that she was nobody's fool.

MISTY MORNINGS, MAGIC NIGHTS
Ada Steward #319—July 1986
The last thing Carole Stockton wanted was to
fall in love with another politician, especially
Donnelly Wakefield. But under a blanket of
secrecy, far from the campaign spotlights,
their love became a powerful force.

COMING NEXT MONTH

THE PERFECT TOUCH—Rita Rainville
Psychologist Jana Cantrell was hired to help reduce the stress at
Wade Master's company. She soon found that Wade was causing
her own tension level to rise.

A SILENT SONG—Lacey Springer
When Gray Matthews rented the apartment upstairs, Allegra
determined to keep her distance. She couldn't risk getting
involved with a man who might discover her true identity... or
could she?

ONCE UPON A TIME—Lucy Gordon
Bronwen was a young widow struggling to care for her son, until
an Italian prince rode into her life proclaiming her son his heir
and capturing her heart as well.

REASON ENOUGH—Arlene James
Captain Vic Dayton had very specific ideas about decorum. Coral
defied every convention that Vic held dear, yet it was her
charming lack of inhibitions that eventually melted his heart.

CROSSWINDS—Curtiss Ann Matlock
Amanda was lovely, spirited, sensual... but she was a minister!
Cole found himself inexplicably drawn to her, but could a man
like Cole actually fall in love with a preacher lady?

BEWITCHED BY LOVE—Brenda Trent
Sweet, vulnerable Ashlyn Elliott was a witch. Playing the sexy
witch Ravenna on television created a dual life for Ashlyn, and
Davis Chamberlain found himself falling in love with both of her.

AVAILABLE THIS MONTH: